HEARTLESS

by Mya Zemlock

Copyright © 2014 by Mya Zemlock

First Edition –February 2014

Front cover illustration by Craig Peterson

ISBN
978-1-4602-3523-2 (Hardcover)
978-1-4602-3524-9 (Paperback)
978-1-4602-3525-6 (eBook)

All rights reserved.

No part of this publication may be reproduced in any form, or by any means, electronic or mechanical, including photocopying, recording, or any information browsing, storage, or retrieval system, without permission in writing from the publisher.

Produced by:

FriesenPress

Suite 300 – 852 Fort Street
Victoria, BC, Canada V8W 1H8

www.friesenpress.com

Distributed to the trade by The Ingram Book Company

PROLOGUE

The world wasn't always like this. There weren't always dead people walking around trying to eat you. I wasn't always the person I am now. Hell no. I used to be goody-two-shoes, straight-A student, animal loving, afraid-of-spiders Alexandra Grason. Now, spiders are the least of my worries. Now, I don't have to worry about school, or friends, or parents. Now, the only thing I have to worry about is myself. Because now, I'm Alex – and at the height of my worries? Ending up like the rest of my family.

Being eaten by zombies.

CHAPTER 1

"Oh, come on!" I said, tossing my spoon back into the sink. Outside, on the short street that held the tiny inn I was in, a flesh-eater was rambling towards the back door. It was obviously male. He had short hair and khaki-colored cargo shorts paired with a muscle shirt. But the muscles that were once shown off with the shirt were now gray and decayed. A brown, crusted gash on his face revealed how he'd become infected. His gray skin hung off of his body like an extra-large shirt on a clothesline.

I sighed. This was the perfect little camp, too. It had running water and electricity, so I could take showers, and drink as much water as I wanted. Well, I guess it was time to pack up.

I took out my canteen and my extra water bottle and refilled them both with cold water. Then, I raided the pantry for anymore non-perishable goods that didn't require a can-opener. You would be surprised at how hard it is to find a manual can-opener nowadays. Pretty near impossible. The only useful things I found were some dried jerky, some peanut butter, and you know those powder drink mixes that you put in a water bottle and shake up and then, voila, you have fruit punch or lemonade or ice tea or something? Yeah, some of those. Those drink pouches have become my favorite item, post-apocalypse.

I also found some bullets for my semi-automatic Glock. I tucked the little box of bullets into the front pouch of my sack. It was essentially a messenger bag that I assumed was used for a book bag. It worked well, but I would have liked something stronger that I could carry on my back. And the messenger bag was a bit small. I had to shove everything in it – everything being the jerky, peanut butter, extra water bottle, bullets, a kitchen knife that I used as a saw, my shotgun, some extra shoes, and a pillowcase that had some extra clothes in it that I rested my head on at night when I was on the run. I usually couldn't find a good place to sleep, so I just slept in the street or under a car.

No biggie.

Using a rubber band, I tied my elbow-length blonde hair back into a ponytail. Back before the whole apocalypse thing happened, I was always the odd one out because of my bright blonde hair and green eyes. Way long ago, like fifty years ago, scientists found out why everybody was reproducing with brown hair and gray eyes. It was because we humans accidentally pushed out all of the people with the recessive traits of light hair colors, so now everybody's hair was dark brown or black. People with light hair were shunned, and left to live alone without anybody. Some people would color their hair blonde just to be different, or to shock people or whatever.

As for the gray eyes, back in the early 2020's it was all the rage to change your eyes to a different color temporarily. You just went to the drugstore and picked a box of your color choice off the shelves. Inside of the box were little eye inserts that were similar to colored contacts, except instead of leaving them in for the color, they would dissolve on your eye and leave behind the color on your irises. People found that after years of using the contacts, they would have children born with gray eyes. They started popping up everywhere, and soon, eighty-percent of the population had gray eyes. Why I had green and my parents didn't I have absolutely no idea. Maybe I'm some weird mutant. That would explain…well…

Let's just say I wasn't very well liked in school.

My mother and father – whom I'd never known since they ran off and were killed when I was a child – were both normal, in terms of society. They were abnormal to me because they left their own child behind, just because they didn't want her – just because she looked different. They both had dark-brown hair, like everyone else. But they were both heterozygous, which means they both had the genes in them of light hair-color and dark hair-color. There had been a one-in-four chance that I would inherit the light hair-color, and guess what? Lucky me, I get light hair. As for the eyes, well, nobody knows. My grandmamma, who was my mother's mother, said that my mother had small specks of green in her eyes, but nobody really noticed, because the rest of her eyes were gray. Why I had to be the one with the weird eyes *and* hair, I have no idea. In school, it caused people to avoid me like the plague.

Once I had everything packed up and ready to go, I remembered that the upstairs bathroom had extra bars of soap. I ran up the stairs two at a time and made a right, down a long, thin hallway. Opening the door to the bathroom, I was hit with the smell of lemon polish. I yanked open the cabinet under the sink and grabbed a soap bar, stuffing it into my bag as I ran back down the stairs and out the back door.

The little inn had been so nice and cool that the heat punched me in the face. It was at least ninety degrees outside and I was happy that I'd remembered to pull back my hair. It was humid, too, which added to the feeling that you were melting. And it was only ten in the morning. I looked down at my thin red flannel. I was tempted to take it off but if I got scratched, then I would turn into a flesh-eater – a zombie, if you will. Then I would really be in trouble.

But the smell, oh the smell! The smell in the city was much worse than in the country, but one tended to get used to it nowadays. The smell of the apocalypse in the summer was worse than a sushi buffet at a gas station. It smelled like rotting flesh and human waste that had been microwaved then hosed down and thrown at your face. I know. Disgusting description, right? Well, that's how it smelled. Add this to the usual disgusting city smell of urine and cigarette smoke and right there you have a good sense of how everything smelled during the apocalypse.

I glanced down the street to look for the male flesh-eater in the khaki shorts that I'd seen earlier and after a bit of walking, I found him behind a green car that had wrecked and overturned. It wasn't very hard to find him though. They like to just hang out in cars. Cars are a good place to wait for people to come along. Then they can eat whatever stupid, unfortunate person struggles along without looking in the cars on the freeway.

He lurched toward me, but I just whipped my Glock out of my waistband and pulled the trigger. The flesh-eater slumped back against the car, officially re-dead. You see, I'd shot him through the brain, so he could no longer move or have a motive to eat people. There must be something in the mushy organ in your head, even when you're dead.

I spun my Glock and tucked it back into my waistband, like a gunslinger or a cowgirl. This town was relatively small. The highway was just two miles from Main Street, if I remembered correctly. It shouldn't take too long to get back on the road. I wasn't really headed anywhere in particular – just away. Away from a history that I didn't want; one that I also missed terribly. I missed waking up in a fresh bed, and knowing that I wasn't going to be facing my worst fears that day. Then again, my school was one of my worst fears, back when I was a wuss. Now I don't care about anything but getting from place to place.

I would walk for a few miles, kill a few flesh-eaters, rest behind a car and do it again – over and over. This process got me through the day. If I started thinking or if I got the least bit distracted, I would trip and fall or almost get eaten. That is how I got a cut in my shoulder a month or two ago. I tripped over a random piece of metal. It healed nicely, a great surprise to me who thought I was going to die just from tetanus or something. That is the trick. In this world, you can die from anything, just having to survive another day.

Most people would find me odd. I mean, other than the fact that I have green eyes and blonde hair. They might see me, and think, "Doesn't she get lonely, walking around in the apocalypse for months on end without ever speaking to another soul?" Yeah. I miss people. But I was never a very popular person in the first place, so I don't necessarily miss socializing with them – just seeing them and knowing that they won't gnaw my fingers off or that I could try talking to them if I wanted to.

At maybe seven or eight o'clock, it was starting to get dark and that was when the flesh-eaters really started to come out to search for their prey. I was still on the highway, so I looked for an exit sign. I found one about a mile down the road, for a town called Penn Hills. The town was still three miles from the road sign, so I decided to make camp for the night. Looking around, I saw a small ditch near the road. I walked over to it carefully, making sure that there were no flesh-eaters anywhere. Looking around once more, I spotted a car just a few yards down the road from where I was standing and decided it would be safer to sleep in the car than in the ditch.

I walked over to the small green car. It looked like one of those weird, little smart cars that became popular in the 2020s. Then people started hating them in the 2030s because they were really unsafe. They were very light because they were made to be fast, so when they collided with a bigger car, they basically exploded.

Prying open the door, I managed to squeeze into the front seat of the squashed car. I slammed the door with a squeak and checked the backseat. I also checked all of the windows, doors, and sunroof. All good. I did an inventory check and then pulled out my improvised pillow. Then I settled in for the night, ready to do it all again tomorrow.

Chapter 2

When I woke up the next day, it was sunrise. So, it was about seven o'clock in the morning. I sighed, then got up and put my pillowcase back into my messenger bag. Another day of survival. Yay for me. I got out my canteen and drank the last of it. Time to break into my water bottle. I also took a piece of beef jerky and scooped out some peanut butter with my fingers.

I would have had a better breakfast if I'd known how to hunt. Grandpapa never got to teach me how before he died when I was seven. And Grandmamma didn't want me hunting after he died either. But Grandpapa did have quite a supply of weapons, I can tell you that. That is where I got my Glocks. I stole them from his study after…before I left. It's best not to delve into the past when there isn't anything too exciting to tell.

With a great creaking sound, I managed to kick open the door of the car. It swung completely off of its hinges and broke off. You could see the outline of my combat boot where I kicked the soft leather of the door. I felt bad that I'd ruined the car and that I'd given another flesh-eater a place to hide but a girl's got to do what a girl's got to do.

Setting off in the direction of Penn Hills, I concentrated on my surroundings. This morning was slightly cooler than the morning before; about seventy degrees at eight o'clock in the morning. It was August, so summer would be ending soon and it was good that it was getting cooler. Maybe it would make the air smell less disgusting.

I doubted it.

Penn Hills was a relatively small town. It had a McDonald's, which was more than I could say for the last town I'd been in. It also had two drugstores, a dollar store, a pizza place, a bank, and a scummy motel. I believe it had a school too, but I hadn't seen one yet. Not that I planned to. One of the best things about the apocalypse – every day is a day off of school.

I headed inside of the dollar store. The best thing about these small towns is that there were fewer people, so there were not as many flesh-eaters to worry about. Nonetheless, I had to kill one inside of the dollar store. It was one of the store employees, still in his purple uniform-vest, stuck living the rest of his zombie life in his dead-end job. I would have wanted somebody to shoot me in the forehead if that ever happened. There was nothing good in the store anyway. But I did take a package of Jolly Ranchers to suck on and some ibuprofen, in case I got a headache or something. It happens.

I headed over to the motel. Breaking in was incredibly easy. I just got the key from the desk in the main office (while killing the zombie-manager in the process…) Inside of the motel was

9

just as scummy as the outside. The room smelled like mothballs, and Grandmamma's homemade glass cleaner. It was relatively clean though – just dusty. And I'm pretty sure if I had wanted to investigate that I'd probably have found a dead body in the closet.

It didn't even have a mini-bar – or a view.

I flipped the deadlock on the door and flopped down on the bed. I drained the last of the water in my water bottle and threw it aside. I'd refill my canteen and the bottle later.

The pillows on the bed were stiff, and the comforter felt as if it were covered in starch. I dragged my pillowcase out of my bag and put it underneath my head. I fell asleep there, in the crummy motel, listening through the paper-thin walls – always alert.

****

A loud CRACK made me spring up from the bed. I dug a Glock out of my bag and armed myself. The door flew open and standing in the doorway was some dude.

He wasn't a flesh-eater. This much was obvious by the way he held himself. He stood ruler-straight with his feet shoulder-width apart – the stance for a gunman. It was dim in the room, so I couldn't see his face, but I assumed he was his twenties or so, from the way he was built. He had lean muscles in his arms and legs that were shown off with shorts and a t-shirt.

"Drop your weapon!" he said, and I was surprised at the sound. It was much higher than I had expected. It wasn't too high though – it was somewhere between medium and high.

I shook my head. "You are the one who barged into *my* room. You drop your weapon!" Surprisingly, I heard the man/boy/person chuckle.

"Touché," he said. "How about this – on three, we both drop our weapons?" I nodded in the dim light. "Okay, one, two... three." Neither of us dropped our weapons. He laughed again.

"Okay," he said. "I have decided that I like you." The man flipped a switch next to the door. It turned on a light over my bed that flickered for a minute before fully activating. "So, who are you?" he asked me. "And what are you doing in the lovely town of Penn Hills?"

The man was not a man after all, as the light revealed. He couldn't have been more than seventeen years old and had long, brown, wavy hair that reached his shoulders. He also had a bit of stubble but it looked as if he had shaved recently. He had a gun slung across his back, and two in his hands. He had combat boots on, like me. It looked like he had a knife tucked into the waistband of his pants and he had a bag that was on the floor beside him that probably had more goodies in it.

I didn't drop my guard. He lowered his hands down to his sides and I just backed up a step. "Okay, then, I'll start first," the boy sighed. "I'm Kale. I am just coming through this tiny little town. I was planning on staying the night in this hotel."

"Then why did you break my door down?" I asked with an edge to my voice.

Kale shrugged. "My room didn't have any food. I was going through all of the rooms and yours was the only one that there wasn't a key for. It was just luck that you happened to be in here." When I raised an eyebrow, he added, "Lucky for me, anyway."

My lip curled up at his flirtation. It was tacky. And distasteful. "Well, there is no food," I said. "So get out." Kale raised his hands with his palms outward and backed up a step, like he was surrendering.

"Hey," he said. "You are the first person I ran into since I ran away from home. It's dead out there. I was just hoping for some company. It gets lonely, if you know what I mean." He winked, and I scowled in disgust. But he was right. He was the first alive person I had encountered since I ran away from home too. Nonetheless, he was still a dirtball.

"No, thanks," I said. "I don't get along well with others."

"I can see that. What if you made an effort?"

I glared at him for a moment and then lowered my gun. He had a point. It could pay off to have company around. "All right," I said, and he grinned.

"Great! Now, which side of the bed are you sleeping on?" He walked into the room and threw his bag next to the sofa. I punched him in the shoulder, hard.

He didn't even flinch. "Hey, take it easy okay? I was just making a joke. I can sleep on the couch if you would like."

"Yeah, you do that."

"Don't be so quick to hate me. Being in a team will be beneficial for both of us, especially if you can punch those zombies as hard as you punched me just now."

I shrugged.

"You aren't very talkative, are you?" he asked me.

"I never really had anybody to talk to before, so I don't quite know what to say to a stranger," I reply truthfully. I'd never had anybody ask me who I was. I was a nobody that everybody knew about; an outcast in the middle of the inner circle.

"How about you start with your name?" he suggested sarcastically.

"My name is Alex," I told him. No more Alexandra. Alex.

"And, how old would you be, Alex?"

"Fifteen."

Kale raised an eyebrow. He drifted over to the sofa and flopped down, a gun beside him. "I'm sixteen. I can't believe that you're only fifteen."

It was now my turn to arch an eyebrow.

"Your hair makes you look older to me. Well, I went to a boarding academy that was essentially a boot camp that got teenagers ready for the military," he said. "So I have a way with the weapons. I can punch somebody pretty hard too. Have you ever even been hunting before?"

I shook my head ruefully.

"Wow. You are a fifteen-year-old in the apocalypse, and you don't know how to hunt. You will have to be taught. Did you bleach it?"

I scrunch my eyebrows together in confusion. "What? Bleach my hair? Absolutely not."

"But your hair is blonde."

I shrug. "I was born blonde. My Grandmamma wouldn't let me dye it brown, either."

"And your eyes! They look…"

"Green. Yeah, they are." I sigh. I have had this conversation far too many times before.

"Guys must have been all over you."

I snort. "Ha. Yeah, okay. No, they were never 'all over me.' I was more of an outcast, if you want to know the truth."

We sat in silence for a few minutes until we heard rain starting to pour down outside. The door was still lying on the floor in front of my bed and we propped it up in the doorway so that we didn't get wet. In hindsight, this was probably very reckless, just putting up a door that the flesh-eaters could knock down, but I felt safe sitting next to Kale, the sixteen-year-old man-boy who'd gone to a boarding school for the military. I didn't think he would take advantage of me, despite his flirtatious remarks. He was just joking.

Then again, I didn't know people, so I didn't know just what he might try to do.

CHAPTER 3

I held first watch because I was fully rested from the night before. Kale had said that he hadn't slept much the day before but I didn't know if he was lying or if he genuinely hadn't sleep. Judging by the snores that started emitting from his mouth the minute his head hit the pillow, I thought it was the latter.

I had never kept guard before. I'd never had to. I'd never had anybody else who needed watching. Sure, I'd stayed awake a few nights when I couldn't find a safe place to sleep but I didn't stay in one place. I just kept walking. It felt weird, just sitting still, awake, when I could have been moving around. I could have just gone and left Kale to the flesh-eaters but I needed the company.

On the other hand, I thought that if I got too attached to someone or I started to trust someone, they might turn into a liability…or a vulnerability. Right about then, they were the same thing.

I decided to leave Kale. I looked around the small motel room for anything useful and couldn't find anything. Using a light tread, I walked around the room, picking up my stuff and packing it into my bag. Slowly, so as not to disturb the sleeping Kale, I moved the door and propped it up on the wall. Then, when I was outside, I put it back up and into place. I whirled around quickly...and ran into what felt like a brick wall.

I pulled out my shotgun and got ready to fire, only to see that it was Kale that I'd run into, not a flesh-eater. I put my arm down and sighed. How the hell had he gotten out there and past me so quickly?

"What are you doing, Blondie?" he asked, knife in hand. It was not aimed in my direction, so I assumed he was not intending to use it on me.

"Don't call me that," I snapped.

"Why are you running?"

I explained quickly. "I didn't want any company."

"Why?"

"Ever heard of personal space?"

"Hey," he said, raising his hands, palms out, as if surrendering. "I let you have your space. It was a matter of social problems that made you uncomfortable."

I glowered at him. "I will use this," I said, motioning towards my gun.

He just laughed and raised an eyebrow. "Really? Hah, you probably never even used that gun on a living person. Probably stole it after you ran away from whatever home that you had. May have even been your father's gun. And aside from a few lucky shots, you probably never shot anything with it either.

Never practiced with it. I can tell, just by the way that you hold it. Your grip is awkward, your fingers turned outward."

I just stood there in silence, my mouth open. He learned all of that about me, just from my gun? I blush and lower my gun so that the barrel is pointed towards the ground. "Just because I don't shoot my gun the same way you do," I said rather quietly, "doesn't mean that I don't know anything about guns, or how to hit my target." Kale hit my weak spot. I built myself up on my strengths, and so when he picked out a weakness my guard crumbled a bit.

Kale grinned and I knew that now we were allies. He turned and started walking and I hesitated a bit before following him. Trusting people was dangerous. You didn't know what was going to happen. Maybe I'd like this Kale boy. He seemed nice enough. And though he was sociable, I could tell that he knew what he was doing. I found a twinge of jealousy hiding behind my stomach. He got to be good at killing people *and* be a people person? So not fair. I threw the shotgun into a pile of rubble nearby and left it.

Kale walked down a street called Juniper that had a drug store, a small pizza place, and some private homes. He went into the drugstore and stuffed the first thing he saw into his bag before walking back out. When he saw me staring at him, he raised an eyebrow.

"What the hell was that?" I asked him.

He laughed. "I do that with every town. I walk into a store, grab the first thing I see that looks interesting or helpful, and walk out. Or go look for more items, if I need them."

"Why, other than taking up space in your pack uselessly?"

He thought for a moment and then shrugged. "It doesn't really matter, does it? I mean, if it helps me sometime along the road, it will be helpful, right?"

I continued to stare at him.

"Do you want to see what I got?"

I shrugged indifferently and he pulled out some nail polish remover. I examined the bottle and saw that it contained acetone. "Why did you grab acetone?" I asked him.

"Can't it be used like rubbing alcohol?"

"I honestly don't know. I never used nail polish remover before."

"Then let's just say yes."

We continued down Juniper Street and hung a left. Right behind the corner of a building, a lurking flesh-eater was hiding behind a blue mail box. I let Kale take it out with his knife and we continued some more. After about ten minutes of walking, we found ourselves on the highway, heading in the direction I'd come from.

I called out. "Kale? I…this is the way I came from."

He turned around and gave another shrug. "All right, then let's go in the other direction. Make life a little more interesting."

We walked down the highway in silence; communication unnecessary. We didn't need to speak to know who was killing what, or what to be careful of. We had both been on our own long enough to know the dangers of the road. Before the apocalypse, you were more likely to be hit by a car on the highway than to be eaten by a crazy lunatic. But hey, you never know.

As we plodded along, I found myself thinking of the origin of the "disease" that created the zombies. It all started when a certain someone, whom am I going to call Zombie Subject #1 started undergoing testing, concerning a treatment for cancer. Ironically, they called the process "Morgue." Nobody really knew the bloody details but the result of the process ended up in a swelled brain, a stopped heart, and the incurable hunger for living, breathing human flesh.

So. Zombie Subject #1 bit one of the research people. The researching scientist became infected. He bit someone, who became infected and bit someone else.

In the span of six months, the entire world's population went from eight billion humans to 7.99 billion zombies.

Kale interrupted my thoughts by abruptly veering toward the left. I drew up my Glock very quickly and looked around before following Kale off to the side, behind a black car.

"What is it?" I asked him.

He put a finger to his lips before looking around again, listening intently, and then pulling himself up off the ground. He offered me his hand but I ignored it, brushing myself off and standing beside him.

He rolled his eyes and brushed himself off as well. "I thought I heard something," he said.

I looked around, not seeing anything but overturned cars. "Do you know how to drive?" I asked him.

He looked at me from the side of his vision. "Of course. Don't you?"

I blushed but I held my head high. "No. I never learned. I was only fourteen when the apocalypse came, and I'm fifteen now."

He gave an audible laugh and I glared at him. "What?" I said.

"You never learned how to drive?"

"Didn't I just say that?" I snapped.

"But it's so utterly simple. Where did you come from?"

I didn't really feel like giving him my whole life story, so I just told him that I came from California. Which was true. I lived in the suburbs of Los Angeles.

"And you got all the way to Colorado without a car?" he asked skeptically.

I shrugged. I had no idea where I was. I just kept moving. Away. Away from my past. On and on and on. Never looking back.

"Wow. I congratulate you. And where are you headed?" he asked.

"Nowhere in particular. Just away."

He nodded. "I understand. I'm headed for the forests."

I raise an eyebrow.

"What?" he asks.

"Why a forest?"

"Well, more of a state park – a place with a small ranger's house or something. It makes sense, when you think about it. More woods, fewer people."

I shrugged. I couldn't have cared less about where I went. But, I guessed I would be following him, now that we were allies. "Which park?" I asked.

"Shenandoah State Park. In Virginia. It's relatively small."

I made no comment, so we continued down the highway, with only the sound of our feet on the pavement between the two of us.

CHAPTER 4

My new ally Kale and I walked on without another word for what seemed to be thirty hours, though it couldn't have been more than twelve. I know I talk a lot about myself and how I didn't like to think when I was walking but it was different when there was somebody else there. You could think and have somebody cover your back when there was a flesh eater gnawing off your face.

I didn't think much about my past life, because I was scared that I might start pitying myself and that was just…well, pitiful. And I didn't want anybody pitying me, because you only pity the weak. Pity was for those who wanted help with everything, or those who needed help with everything, even though they might not want it.

I started thinking about hot fudge sundaes, and peanut butter and jelly sandwiches, and bananas. Oh, how I missed bananas, or any fresh produce for that matter. I wouldn't have been surprised if I'd gotten scurvy, had I not been walking in the sun all day and every day for five months.

Getting back to reality, I was still walking when Kale stopped, so he had to grab onto my arm to stop me from falling over a large piece of metal...again.

"Alex!" he scolded. I turned to face him, my head high in the air, yet a slight blush on my cheeks. "You need to watch where you are going, for the fifth damn time!"

"I realize this," I told him evenly. He didn't need to remind me every time I did something wrong. It gets annoying.

"Obviously," he spat. He turned away, and I childishly mimed his scolding of me under my breath. Sometimes I felt like wringing his stupid, tan neck. We both asserted far too much authority. It was like that, "This town's too small for the both of us," kind of thing, which was ironic considering that the only towns I'd been in, all of the other people were dead.

At dusk we stopped to eat and sleep. I decided to take first watch because I'd tried to skip out on Kale and I felt bad. Kale slept inside of a small car while I sat on the roof, guarding his sleeping figure. I could have easily tried to leave him to the flesh eaters again, but he was turning out to be good company...most of the time.

I had to shoot one or two flesh eaters that tried to sneak up on Kale, and he didn't even turn in his sleep. That guy was such a heavy sleeper that I would not have been surprised if he slept till dawn. And I have no doubt in my mind that he would have, if I hadn't woken him up a few hours before it. It was probably four in the morning when I rolled him out of the car.

"Why am I on the ground?" he asked me, his groggy words slightly slurred.

I stifled a laugh. "The flesh-eaters were trying to drag you out."

"Aw man..."

This time, I really did laugh. "It's okay though. I fought 'em off. It was also me who dragged you out of the car to wake you up."

"Why?"

"Dude," I said. "You were snoring so loud that if it were me, I would have woken myself up."

"That happens sometimes."

"What? You sleep through anything?"

"Yup. Often, when I've been walking far."

I nodded in agreement. Before the apocalypse, I would have been dead on my feet after walking so far – pun not intended. But since I'd walked so far every day by then, I just recharged in my sleep. It made life so much easier for me and my feet.

By the time Kale was walking around and eating his meager breakfast of beef strips and water, the sun was starting to break over the horizon. This made me nervous; staying in one place out in the open for so long. But it looked like there wasn't any way to rush Kale. Kale went when Kale felt like going.

The temperature was rising steadily. After the cool snap, summer was coming back again, with full force, and just the thought of it made me cringe. Warm temperatures equaled more revealing clothes, more sweat, or both. Zombies loved the combination.

We continued east, stopping for what I like to call a "pee and tea" break. I peed in the woods, or a ditch, or behind a car

– somewhere – then I took one of the dried fruits, crushed it up (with some mint leaves if I was lucky), then put it in some water to make "tea." More like "flavored water with dried fruit chunks," but a beggar can't be a chooser, and I took what I could get.

Kale didn't eat anything, even though I offered him some dried fruit. He claimed that he wasn't hungry yet and that was understandable. In long stretches between supply stops in town, my stomach had probably shrunk to the size of a walnut over the past five months. Not having anything to eat for almost a whole day didn't bother me any more.

We were both resting in the shade of a shipping truck when Kale asked me, "Do you miss anything?"

I laughed, but was taken aback by his question. "Of course I miss things. I'm not a robot, am I?" I checked my arms and legs, pretending to make sure.

"Hah, I guess. I don't miss much of it, though. I didn't have a great life."

"Me neither," I said. "I miss the fresh food and waking up in a warm bed."

"I miss waking up and not worrying about being killed."

"Hah, yeah. I guess I miss that too."

"Do you miss your family, though?"

This question seemed a bit personal, so I lied, "Not much."

"The only person in my family I miss is my brother." He stopped talking suddenly, as if lost in thought.

I continued, pretending not to notice. "I'm an only child. Well, I think I am."

"What do you mean?"

"Well, I grew up with my Grandmamma, and I never met my parents. I don't remember them, at least."

"So you don't know if you have any brothers or sisters?"

"Nope." I didn't think I did though. I was pretty sure I'd been an accident in the first place. I mean, I lived with my grandmother! Wasn't that proof enough?

"What about friends and stuff?" he asked.

I laughed. "None. I was quite the reject."

"Because of your hair? That's a sucky reason. Everyone in my school hated the people who bleached their hair. I would be like, 'piss off,' you know?"

"Yeah. I know."

We stopped talking after that.

Walking along, I realized that in two short days, Kale had become my friend. Anybody who knew that much about me had to be a friend. Probably the first real friend I'd had.

CHAPTER 5

We did the same thing every day for three weeks. Walk, kill a few flesh eaters, then we would switch with each other for night shift. Surprisingly, we were a good team. Kale took the front, while I snuck around and blew the flesh-eaters' brains apart. At this rate, we would be absolutely indestructible....

...until we started fighting each other. Apparently, I had a long lost brother, because Kale and I fought like we were siblings. About impractical things, too, like the way I grip my gun and the way he shuffles his feet when he walks.

I believe we were on a highway somewhere in Kansas. It was Kale's turn to keep watch but I couldn't sleep. I was restless. So I was sitting on the hood of the car with Kale when we heard two gunshots. Ducking reflexively, we slid off the hood of the car and crouched behind it. We were just pulling out our guns when we heard a high, female shriek.

I jumped up and ran off in the direction of the scream – Kale calling out in protest. When I found the source, I gasped.

Five or six flesh-eaters were surrounding a young girl who couldn't have been more than fourteen. She was gasping in horror, too terrified to scream for help. She was trying to aim a shotgun into the horde, and was only hitting arms and abdomens.

I helped her out. Getting low, I ran through the horde with my arms out wide, a knife in each hand. I heard a bloody *schlock!* – as my knives connected with the gray slabs of meat that were the flesh-eaters' legs and some of them fell. Once I got inside to the girl, I shielded her behind my legs and used my Glocks to shoot into the horde. There were gunshots somewhere to my right and I assumed it was Kale. I took shot after shot, hitting some in the eyes, and some in the cheek or temple. They all went down.

We were splattered with reddish-black gore and there were carcasses lying on the ground. I looked behind me to see the girl staring at me in awe. She had short, brown hair that went to the middle of her neck. I assumed that she'd hacked it off herself because it was choppy and uneven.

This took me by surprise, considering I could just tell by her demeanor and her cries for help that she was the "girly and defenseless" type. I couldn't even bring myself to cut an inch off of my hair, despite the heat and the dangers of it becoming snagged and trapping me. It wasn't like I adored my hair or anything. It had constantly gotten me into fights and I was never well-liked because of it. It had caused me to become an outcast. But my hair was like a part of who I was. It stood as a reminder of what I had been through and what I could take – how weak I was. It was a part of who I was.

The girl was still staring at me, though it must have been at least thirty seconds by then. I guess I was still looking at her though, so I could let her off the hook. She seemed to be in shock, her gray eyes becoming nickels as she stared at me with admiration and fear.

I turned to the right and saw, not Kale, but another boy. He had longish brown hair that must have tickled his eyelids when he blinked. His gray eyes were darker than the girl's and his features were soft, like hers. I immediately realized that they must have been siblings. His long sleeved T-shirt and blue jeans were ragged and covered in dirt and grime. I saw the faint glint of a thin gold necklace around his neck as he wiped off two long blades that looked like broadswords, but were far too small to actually be them. He tucked them into two leather holsters at his waist.

"Who are you?" the girl asked me, and I realized that I was staring at the boy.

I looked at her, still on the ground. "Alex," I said shortly.

The boy walked forward and took my hand, giving it two awkward shakes. "I'm Nate," he said, "and this is my sister, Lynne."

"Awesome," I said, turning away and walking angrily in the direction of where Kale was hiding. He could have helped us protect this girl and instead he hid behind a car?

Coward.

"Wait!" Nate yelled and he tried to catch up to my brisk pace. "Where are you going? Can we at least thank you before you walk off?"

"You're welcome," I said, and continued walking. The girl, Lynne, seemed to be running to catch up.

"Are you just leaving then?" Nate asked me and I shook my head.

"No, I'm getting my ally and beating his ass for not helping us out."

"You have an ally?" he asked, and I ignored the question. They'd meet each other soon enough.

"Kale, you asshole!" I yelled when I got to the car. He stood slowly and I shoved him.

He shoved me back. "What Alex? You just risked your life for some pretty boy and this useless little girl?"

"They needed help," I said through gritted teeth.

"And that wasn't our problem," Kale retorted.

"The human welfare is our problem. What's left of it, anyway."

"Exactly. What's left of it. This means we can't afford to be risking strong people for weak little girls."

"All people are worth saving. You just have to find the good that is in them to see that."

"Thinking like that is going to get you killed. There are people out there that would not hesitate to shoot you right now. Do you realize that? You can't exactly find the good in people when you are dead."

"And they would probably both be dead right now, if it weren't for me. I would like them to see the good in me, too, and for them to hopefully help me if I ever need it. Would you do that Kale? Because I really don't think you would."

We stood there glaring at each other for a few tense seconds until Nate stepped between us. "I agree with...Alex, was it?"

I gave a terse nod, and he stuck a hand out to Kale. "Hey, I'm Nate. And that girl over there that 'isn't worth saving' is my sister, Lynne. So you might just want to watch what you say about her around me."

Kale just turned and looked for Lynne, and when he spotted her, he curled his lip in disgust. Nate dropped his hand back to his side.

"How did you get so close?" Kale asked Nate suspiciously. "Have you been following us?"

"No!" Nate exclaimed. "We just got on the highway an hour ago, after coming out of Topeka. We had to make a break for it and I think the night-walkers followed us."

"Topeka?" I asked. "Isn't that near the center of the state? And why would you go to a city? Flesh-eaters are abundant in cities."

After a few moments, Nate finally said, "…I guess. And I don't know geography very well, so maybe."

By now, Lynne had caught up, breathing hard. I rolled my eyes. She was a bit weak.

"Good. Where are you going?" I asked them, hoping they were not headed in the same direction as us.

"Oh, nowhere in particular," Lynne said in a cheery, high-pitched voice.

Oh, that would get annoying very quickly.

"Great. Well, we'll be on our way." I turned and started walking, because by now the sun was breaking the horizon, glaring at us with its harsh, orange rays. Kale walked beside me, gun still drawn.

"Wait!" both Lynne and Nate called and they ran in front of us, stopping us from continuing. "Why don't we come with you?"

Kale and I looked at each other. I shrugged, showing my indifference, and he shook his head. Meanwhile, the other two were looking at us like we were lunatics.

Still looking directly at Kale, I said, "You can come with us. But everyone pulls their own weight."

"Deal," Nate agreed, and we headed east once more. Toward what? We didn't quite know yet.

****

We had only been walking in silence for about half an hour before Lynne stated that it was too quiet. So she and Nate dropped back behind us to talk, apparently about their new companions. They had been talking for a good five or six minutes before I heard my name and started to eavesdrop.

"She is nice…" This came from Lynne.

"She's okay, but I don't trust that other guy. Kale, I think she said his name was?"

"He just needs time to adjust."

"Alex didn't." Nate sounded a bit gruff, uncomfortable. I smirked.

"Everybody's different."

"And? What do you think they meant to do if we didn't insist on coming along with them? Go off and join a zombie-killing biker gang?"

"Don't be mean. They probably had rough lives." Lynne paused. "And hey, what do you know, that Alex girl is kind of pretty."

"Sure," Nate replied. "But what's with her hair?"

"It's blonde. She probably bleached it."

"I like it. It's…different."

I stopped listening because by now there was a blush on my cheeks, and if Kale saw, he would ask about it. I glanced at him out of the corner of my eye, and saw him smirking. I punched him on the shoulder and he wiped it off his face. My cheeks felt like a furnace by now.

It was sweltering. I'm pretty sure it was September, both by the temperature and the amount of time that had passed. I had been on the run for five whole months. In that time, the only human beings that I'd seen were me, myself, and I. And some motel manager, but that's another story. Until three weeks ago… when I met Kale, and he became my friend…And now? three companions? I thought two was pushing it. The more flesh, the more flesh-eaters. In fact, here were some now.

"Guys, in position. Or, just stand your ground. Kale, I'll take the back." He nodded at me, and I snuck behind a burnt-out car. It blocked my view of Kale and the other two but I could see the flesh eaters perfectly. There seemed to be around ten, nothing we couldn't handle. I snuck around to the back of the horde, car by car.

I got behind them and counted to three. One breath – two steps – three shots. Go.

I used my knives to injure the zombies' legs first. This hobbles them and makes them easier to kill. I heard gunshots and had no reason to panic. If someone was going to shoot them, it was going to be Kale.

I got out my guns and shot them alternately. There were only one or two flesh eaters left, so I backed away slowly, keeping my eyes on them, just in case they decided to turn on me. Out of the corner of my eye, I saw Lynne get out her shotgun. I just had time to dive to the side and avoid the bullet. A searing, burning pain spread slowly up my arm. Gritting my teeth, I looked up to see Kale shouting at the poor girl, and Nate hacking at the flesh eaters with his knives.

When the last two were dead and lying on the ground, limbs hacked apart, I jumped up and checked myself for injuries. Lynne's bullet seemed to have skimmed the back of my right arm. It was bleeding, not too badly but more than when I got cut on that piece of metal.

I took my guns and walked over to where Nate, Lynne, and Kale were standing. Kale and Nate seemed to have gotten into an argument and Lynne's eyes shone with tears.

I pointed to her. "Are you the one who shot me?"

She gaped like a fish. "I-I didn't know any bullets hit you," she stuttered.

I could tell she was scared. She was almost wetting her pants. I looked at Kale and he was trying to hide a smirk. I suddenly start smirking too and then burst out laughing. Kale joined in with a small chuckle, while the shaking Lynne and the shocked Nate just stared.

"You were so scared!" I shouted, doubling over and clutching my stomach. "You thought I was going to – to yell at you or something!" By now I was gasping for air and wiping the tears from my eyes.

Nate spoke up. "That's not funny! You've terrified her!"

"And she shot me," I laughed back. "Come on, it's just a…"

Kale interrupted. "You really did get shot?"

I nodded. "Yeah, it's just a flesh-wound, though." I showed them the blood running down my arm and realized it was getting thicker. "Aw shoot," I said, unbuttoning my flannel and laying it on the ground at my feet. The blood was running down my arm, and some of it got on my gray tank top that I wear underneath.

"Are you okay?" asked Nate.

I looked up at him and saw the concern in his eyes. "Yes…" I said slowly; confused. Why was he worried about me, a girl he met not an hour ago? "I just need something to bind this with. Does anybody have anything I can use?" They all searched through their bags until Lynne came up with a white, long-sleeved sweater. I took it from her trembling hands and then sat on the hood of a car to wrap it.

First I used the sweater to mop up some of the blood off of my arm. I winced when I prodded the surrounding skin – the pain finally registering. Kale gave me the acetone from his bag so that I could clean my hands and the wound better. I soaked part of the sweater with acetone and then clenched my jaw as I pressed the alcohol-based chemical to my arm, hard. I had to grit my teeth to keep myself from screaming. Bullet wounds are painful, regardless. But putting alcohol on them makes the pain intensify. Ten-fold. Once I had the wound clean, I attempted to wrap it. It was too hard, though, considering I was wrapping my own arm.

"Here, let me help you with that," Nate said. He used the sweater to wrap my arm, and one of Lynne's bobby pins to keep it in place.

"Thank you," I said, and he just nodded his head. I walked back over to my flannel. It was drenched with blood. I thought about attempting to put it on, but that would be painful, so I just left it off. I turned around to face my companions, the new and the newer. "Are we ready to blow this pop stand?"

They all grinned at one another, before Kale said for all of us, "Hell yeah."

CHAPTER 6

We stuck to the highway for about a week, and let me tell you, my bleeding arm attracted lots of flesh eaters. We all tried fighting in twos. Usually, it was Kale and I, and Nate and Lynne. Nate could really fight with those knives. His skill made up for Lynne's lack thereof.

Sometimes, Kale and Nate would go together, or Nate and I. Neither Kale nor I wanted to team up with Lynne. She was clumsy, and I was surprised she hadn't shot anybody before.

We also learned a lot about our new companions. Nate was sixteen, like Kale, and his sister was as I guessed, fourteen. Lynne was really, really girly. She had a few skirts in her bag, and a black, flouncy dress. Her shoes were sparkly, pink winter boots. She sometimes liked to spray perfume on herself when she thought she smelled worse than usual. But that girly, soft exterior had a pretty hard interior. She didn't deal with crap. She chopped her hair off when it got to be about the same length as mine because she didn't feel like dealing with it. She liked the feel of a gun in her hand, even if she was terrible at shooting.

Nate was pretty much a typical guy. He didn't have any special qualities that I knew of, except for being able to crack a great joke now and then. Though he was great with knives. When I asked him where he learned to fight with knives like that, he shrugged and said that it just came naturally.

We decided to take an exit off of the highway when we saw the name of another city that we recognized – Jefferson City, the capital of Missouri.

"We should probably avoid the city," I said, thinking aloud. They all nodded in agreement.

"Topeka was terrible," said Lynne, whose quavering voice was accompanied by a full body shudder. "There were roamers everywhere!"

"Well, duh," I said, whilst rolling my eyes. "The more people there were in one place, the more flesh-eaters that are there now."

We took an exit on our left that was labeled with the name "Wardsville." Walking through, I made a note to myself that it was a fairly small town. It wasn't as small as Penn Hills but it was still pretty small, considering it didn't even have a minimall. The limited stores consisted of a variety of the usual; a pizza place, a hotel, a McDonalds, a family-run grocery store, and a small gas station. It also had an ice cream shop. Yum.

I was most excited to see the store that a sign overhead identified as "Mike's Hunting Gear and Weaponry." I didn't know who or what Mike was now, but I would thank him later.

We busted into the weapons shop and I immediately took out two flesh-eaters. Maybe they worked there once. I didn't know and I honestly didn't care at this point.

Along the walls was an endless supply of camouflage, guns, tree-stand seats, knives, bows, arrows, and bullets. We all browsed through the shop, picking up whatever, as my Grandmamma used to say, 'Tickled our fancies.'

I saw a set of hunting knives that were a bit long, maybe the length of my forearm. I called Kale over to show him and he took a set as well. He also picked up a small dagger that had a red spade on the handle, and pocketed it.

Lynne was browsing through the store's bags, so I decided to join her. They had a small selection, mostly duffel bags and the mesh game bags. There was one book bag that was pink and black camouflage. She picked it up and looked at it, and I let her have it. Pink was definitely not my color.

Nate was looking at guns. He picked one up, looked at it, and then put it back. I chuckled and walked over to him. After looking over the array of firearms, I found one that closely resembled my Glocks and handed it to him. "Here, use this."

He looked at it and shook his head. "I don't do guns."

"Think of it as a backup," I said, and put it in his pack with three boxes of bullets. I got three boxes for myself as well. "Are we ready to go?" I asked everybody, and they all nodded. "Onward, then."

We stopped by the clothing store to pick up some new, not grungy-and-stained-with-gore outfits. I found a purple tank top and white flannel. I changed into the tank top in the dressing room and shoved the new flannel into my bag, throwing the old one out. I also wiggled myself into a pair of skinny jeans, put my combat boots back on, and laced them up. I shoved an extra pair of socks into my pillowcase with the flannel and then walked outside. The bell above the door jingled, so they would know I left. I hoped.

The McDonalds was on my right so I stopped there to see if they had any good food left. I jumped behind the counter and searched for food. Unfortunately, it looked like the McDonalds had lost power near the time the apocalypse started and I was not going into that freezer. But beneath the counter were a few bags of those cookie things that they used to put in the kids meals. I grabbed eight bags and shoved them into my pack for later.

As I walked back into the street, there was someone right there. I jumped two steps back and drew my gun.

It was just Nate.

"What are you doing?" he asked, tugging on my arm. He pulled me back towards the clothing store.

I rolled my eyes. "I was right next door."

"No, there was a fight in the store!"

"Then why did you leave?"

"We got them all," he said with an irritated sigh. "We just couldn't find you."

His already tight grip became downright painful, and I shook him off. "I'm fine, thanks." We started walking back to the store. "Besides, why would it matter if a flesh-eater got me? It's not like you know me." I turned to face him.

His cheeks were bright red. "I'm not very good with deaths." He looked down and shuffled his feet a bit, scattering about tiny pieces of what used to be the road.

I shrugged. "Hell, none of us are. We all hate it. But that's a fact of life, I guess. It was even before this whole mess."

We got back to the clothing store and the door clanged open. "Alex! Oh my God, you're okay! I never thought..." Lynne started shouting.

She threw her arms around me and I pried them off. "Easy there, tiger," I interrupted. "I'm fine. You just calm down there."

"I'm sorry. I was just so worried..."

"Why does everybody care what happens to me, and not trust me to protect myself?" I yelled. Lynne stopped blubbering. "I'm not your family, or even your friend. I have been traveling with you a week, and have been on my own for months! I can take care of myself. So lay off!" I turned on my heel and walked away, fuming. I supposed they believed that I couldn't fend for myself? I had been alone much longer than any of them, let me tell you.

Kale ran to catch up to me. "Alex, they're just worried. They think of you as a good companion, if not a friend."

"Really? Me? The snarky girl who doesn't talk unless barking orders. A good companion. Yeah, right."

"Or a friend. You don't think about their feelings, Alex. About what they have been through."

"But they aren't my friends," I said, my voice low. "And it isn't like they're your friends either! You were all for just leaving them behind for the flesh-eaters to get to them, and you want to accuse *me* of not thinking about their feelings or what they have been through? Are you *serious?*"

"I admitted that I was wrong in what I said and apologized already. They accepted and we agreed to try to get along in the future, and now we are on the road to becoming good friends. I know they can be…a hassle, sometimes, but they are your friend." He paused. "Do you even know what a friend is? A friend is someone you can trust. And you can trust us not to put a bullet in your back, don't you?"

I thought about his assessment. "I guess," I mumbled.

"Good. Now let's apologize."

"I'm not apologizing for something like this."

"That's okay. I already did it for you."

I shot him a glare.

He chuckled. "What? Someone had to, and I had already figured that it wouldn't be you."

God, he knew me so well already. I stomped back to where Nate and Lynne were speaking to each other in hushed tones. They were sitting on the counter where the cash register used to reside. Now it seemed to be on the floor behind it. Lynne looked on the verge of tears, as usual. "Crybaby," I muttered under my breath.

Nate apparently heard me, because he whipped his head up and glared at me. "Did it ever occur to you that some are not as physically or emotionally strong as you, Miss Perfect?"

I stopped in my tracks. "I'm not perfect."

"Maybe not, but you act like you are."

I turned on him, my teeth bared. "Say it again. I dare you. I will wipe that smirk off your face."

He looked me straight in the eyes, and said, "Miss. Perfect."

He got a hard smack across his face and I turned away with a smirk of my own. Kneeling down beside Lynne, I said, "I'm sorry. That was out of line."

She just nodded. "Thank you."

I gave her a nod in return. Walking deeper into the store, I surveyed the damage. Three flesh-eaters- nothing that they couldn't handle.

I'm going to tell you something. I was more of an act now-think later kind of person. I couldn't help it. When I was fighting, I didn't have to think about it. My body knew what to do, and then I just ran through the motions. Actually, I intentionally kept my mind blank when fighting. Everything went perfect then.

CHAPTER 7

Out of the corner of my eye, I saw something move. I whipped out my Glock and pointed it in the direction of the movement, searching for any signs of life – or just movement, really. The clothing rack moved again and I shot a round into the fabric and the base of the rack. I heard a squeal, and the rack moved again.

"What in the…"

I moved the racks and shook them to see what was in them. Looking through the clothes, I found a squirrel in the middle of the clothing and twisted metal. It had a bullet hole through its neck. I picked it up by the tail and took it outside. "Hey guys, I've had rabbit, but can we eat this?"

Nate and Kale looked up to the squirrel that was twitching and dangling by its tail, which was in my hand. Nate had a distinct, red handprint on his cheek. I grinned.

"Yeah," said Kale. "You can eat squirrel. I've skinned and cooked them before. Do you want me to do that now?"

I looked around. "Not here. Let's go find a house."

Three streets down was a red-brown, brick house that looked pretty small. I stepped inside and saw that everything was a shade of ashy gray or black. My nose felt on fire as I smelled the ash and smoke. My eyes started to water.

"Oh, wow," said Lynne, who still looked a little green around the edges, presumably from overhearing our conversation about eating the squirrel. "What happened in here?"

Nate coughed. "This is weird…I've never seen a burnt house."

"And why didn't the rest of the house burn down with it?" I ask.

We all looked at each other and shrugged. Why question a good thing? Kale started a fire in the ashes of what I assumed was an upstairs bedroom that had collapsed in the fire. Despite the black and smoky interior, the house seemed pretty stable. We explored the house carefully to find that the staircase that leads to the second-floor was still intact. Just to the right of the landing at the top, we see a large hole, and underneath it is the room that had collapsed from the fire. The rest of the upstairs was untouched by the destructive that had charred the rest of the house.

"Should we just stay here?" Lynne asked.

Nate nodded. "The ashes and smoke will cover our scent."

Kale looked surprised. "He's right," he agreed.

I had to stifle a laugh.

Lynne and I took a bedroom on the top floor. It had a queen bed, a dresser, a small closet, and a desk.

I took the comforter and a pillow off of the bed. Spreading out the comforter at the foot of the bed, I put the pillow on top and laid my pack next to it.

"What are you doing?" asked a voice.

I jumped and pulled my gun, but it was just Lynne. "Don't sneak up on me like that!" I scolded, punching her hard on the shoulder.

She stepped back and put her hands out in front of her. "Sorry, sorry. No need for the bruising, though, ouch." She chuckled and winced as she checked out the fist-shaped red mark on her arm. "You could probably kill them all off with just your fists. Holy cow!"

Now it was my turn to laugh. "I'll keep that in mind if I ever want my hand to be eaten off." We both chuckled for a bit, and I realized that Lynne's high-pitched, tinkling laugh had become less annoying, and more comforting. Like fairy bells in the night, or the jingling of bells. Like home.

Once more, I took an inventory of the items I had in my pack. My food stash was on a shortage, but I still had plenty of the drink packets left. I took one out, shook it to assure that the pink powder would be at the bottom of the package, and ripped the top off with my teeth. I emptied the contents of the packet into my water bottle, screwed on the lid, and then shook it hard for a few seconds. When I took a sip, I realized that Lynne was staring at me.

"What?" I asked her. I held out a packet. "Do you want one?"

She shrugged and took one but didn't use it. She just put it in her new, pink book bag, for later, I supposed.

I tried to forget that she was still staring at me and started playing with the wrapper on my water bottle, which I should have taken off days ago. I needed a new water bottle anyway. When I glanced upward I saw that Lynne was still staring at me. "What?" I demanded of her once more – an edge in my voice.

I guess she could tell that I was disgruntled by her stares, so she apologized. "Sorry. I was just staring at your hair. Why did you bleach it?"

I sighed. "Unfortunately, I didn't. It's just like this." A puzzled look came across her face, so I explained it to her in a flat voice.

"And your eyes?"

I shrugged. "I dunno about those. Neither of my parents had completely green eyes. My mother had flecks but that was it. Or that's what I am told."

She giggled and it's my turn to stare at her. "I like it," she said finally, before another giggle erupted from her lips.

I shook my head and settled down onto my pillow. Lynne muttered something about her brother, and I finally got it. They had been talking about my hair when they first joined us, and had Nate said that he liked it. Suppressing a giggle myself, I got up to go check on the guys with Lynne jumping off the bed and following me.

Kale saw me walk into the makeshift kitchen and said, "Perfect timing." He handed me a bowl of soup. The broth was a very light yellow-brown, and very thin. The only other thing in it other than the squirrel meat seemed to be some small, round noodles that I could only classify as wheels.

I inhaled the stew, slurping it down without any utensils. This was the first fresh meat that I'd had in five months.

Everybody else had to do without spoons as well, and Lynne looked like she wanted to pass on the stew because of this. She saw me and blushed, so I shook my head and put my bowl on the floor. I returned with a small spork that had been in my bag for emergencies, and she thanked me with a nod.

"That was good," Nate said, breaking the silence after around five minutes. We all nodded in agreement. I yawned.

"Yes, thank you, Kale," I said. "But now I'm headed off to bed."

"I think I'll hit the hay, too," Nate said. His room was right next to Lynne and mine's and he let me walk up the stairs first. "After you, miss," he said, and I rolled my eyes. I walked up and bid him goodnight before lying down and falling asleep as my head hit the pillow.

****

I woke up at the crack of dawn, the sun still climbing its way slowly over the horizon. Stretching out my muscles, I got up and walked out of the room, trying to be careful and not wake Lynne. The door creaked open and I winced. I looked back to see her tossing in her sleep. When I had successfully tiptoed out without waking her, I ran into somebody in the hall.

"Sorry," they said, and I looked up to see that it was just Nate. "You have to stop running into me," he whispered with a slight chuckle. I gave a reluctant grin and socked him on the arm. "And quit hitting me!"

I stifled my laugh by putting my hand over my mouth, and Nate laughed with me. "Where are you going?" he asked me. I just shrugged. "Follow me," he said and walked down the stairs to what used to be the kitchen.

After he turned his back to me, I blinked in surprise. While I hated to admit this to myself, I was actually surprised that Nate was being so nice to me, especially after I'd left a red mark on his face that was in the shape of my hand. He forgave too easily.

Nate pried open a door that I hadn't noticed was there before. It was behind the ashes of the counters and pieces of blackened metal. He helped me step over the metal and get my footing.

Behind the door was a set of wooden stairs. They were completely unharmed by the fire, much like the upstairs bedrooms. Nate tried to take my hand and help me down the stairs but I removed my hand from his grip. I didn't need help, although he must have thought me a vulnerable little girl.

When we get to the bottom of the stairs, we made a left down a small hallway. At the end of the hallway was another door. He opened it and I got a waft of musty books before we entered the room. I gasped when I saw what was inside.

"Amazing, isn't it?" Nate asked, his arm swinging wide, showing off his discovery of a small library that had to have had hundreds of books, new and old. I turned in a small circle, taking in the walls that were filled to the top with books. In the corner were a few squashed-looking beanbag chairs and a small desk.

"How did you find this?" I asked him while trailing my fingers over the spines of the old books.

"I went exploring last night."

"It's wonderful!" I said, picking up a book, *Fahrenheit 451*, off of the shelf. "This book is over a hundred years old. And what a coincidence." I laughed. "*Fahrenheit 451*, the first book I pick up, and it's in a burnt house."

"Do you like to read?" asked Nate.

I nodded my head vigorously. "It's all that I used to do. I actually used to work in a library but when the BiblioHolos came to be, nobody went there. So I just sat among the stacks of books and read." This was true but mostly the reason I read so much was because I didn't have anyone to speak with or anything to do. My books were my companions; the characters, my friends; their adventures, my guide. "I obviously don't read much now, from the whole zombie apocalypse and whatnot."

"I personally liked books better than the BiblioHolos."

"I was impartial. A book was a book to me." I took my book and sat on a blue beanbag chair.

"The BiblioHolos weren't my favorite. Of course, I could never afford one anyway so that's probably why I pretended that I didn't want one." He chuckled and sat on a red beanbag that was across from me.

"Like I said, a book was a book. You don't need fancy gadgets to read a book." We sat in silence for a few moments before Nate looked up.

"Did you ever feel like…like you had a connection to a book you were reading? Like the main character's pain, was your pain? And their happiness made you glow too?" He looked uncomfortable, so I put a hand on his arm.

"Of course. Why would somebody read a fiction book, so that they could just say they read it?" He shrugged, and I continued. "Books were made not only for your enjoyment but so that you could do something that you have never done. Experience something you never had – feel a feeling that was never there before. Books help you find out more about yourself. Books help you get away from yourself. Books take you into a new adventure with different people. Books take your mind off of your real problems and give you new ones that you will always triumph over. Books are what happen when your imagination runs wild." I ended my speech and Nate was staring at me, a confused look on his face.

"What is it with you and your sister, always staring at me? First it's my freaking hair and now it's my love of books. I mean, come on!"

Nate laughed and shook his head. "No, no! It's not that, it's just…you're just…inspiring."

I gave him a look that said *Quit making fun of me, jerkoff.*

"You're so…enthusiastic? No, that's not the right word…. Passionate. You are very passionate about books."

"I guess. Books were my only friend."

Nate gave me a look that said he understood and I believed him. He looked like he'd had a rough life, just like me. Well, maybe not to the same extent but probably pretty close.

"O-kaayyy, so, changing topics." I took a breath. "I'm sorry for slapping you, although you kind of deserved it." My apology came out quickly and sounded insincere, making my cheeks flood with pink.

Nate started to laugh, and I had to shush him to remind him that it was just after dawn and that our friends were asleep. He quieted his booming laugh into a slight chuckle. "You're fine, you're fine. I did deserve that though. But a little warning may have helped."

"I did warn you," I pointed out. "When I said that I would wipe that smirk off of your face?"

"I guess that does qualify." We both start laughing again, and now we just couldn't help it. Our laughs made their way upstairs and into the upstairs bedrooms, where we woke Kale and Lynne. They came bursting into the basement's library, Kale with his knives out and Lynne with a baseball bat. When they saw us laughing in the corner, they looked at us with their sleepy eyes and confused looks on their faces.

"What's so funny?" asked Lynne, groggy yet bright.

Nate and I just shook our heads because first of all, we couldn't speak, and second of all, we didn't have an answer, even if we could have told them. It took us both a whole five minutes to calm down enough to breathe, and even then, giggles interrupted our deep, gasping breaths.

"You two are so weird," said Kale, and he put his knives back into his hip holsters. He and Lynne walked back upstairs to the kitchen, leaving Nate and I alone again. He got up off of his beanbag and gave me a hand to help me up as well.

"Thanks," I said.

"Yup."

We headed back up the stairs and we were almost in the kitchen before I remembered the old book in my hand. "Shoot," I said, and Nate turned to see what was wrong. I held up the book. "I have to go put this back."

"Why don't you just keep it to read?" he asked, and I shook my head.

"That library is a paradise in this hell-hole. I don't want to spoil something as special as that by taking something with me." I didn't wait for his response before I turned around and walked back into the underground library to put the book back. I caught back up to him, and he was looking at me weird, once again.

"Seriously, why does everybody stare at me?" I asked him, a bit irritated now. I pushed past him, and he tried to explain.

"You're just so…different."

"Yeah, I've noticed that long ago. Thanks for the reminder."

CHAPTER 8

I found Lynne back in our room, re-packing her bag. "Are we leaving?" I asked her dubiously.

"I'm just packing. In case we have to move soon."

I nodded, and we remained silent for a few minutes. I walked over to my makeshift bed and shoved my pillowcase back into my pack while making sure I still had everything. We could have left in a moment's notice, at any time. Living life on the run wasn't always fun.

When I knew I had everything packed, I left Lynne in the room and walked back into the charred kitchen. Nate and Kale were sitting on something large and metal, and I didn't feel like asking what it was. I sat beside them on the ground.

Kale eyed me suspiciously, for no apparent reason. "What do you want?" he asked me coldly.

I put my hands up, palms out, suggesting innocence. "I can't sit here? Wow, it's like the high school cafeteria all over again."

Nate chuckled. "He's angry that we woke him up."

"Ah. Well, Mr. Grumpy, it isn't my fault that you sleep like a freaking bear."

"Obviously not," Kale retorted, "since you and Mr. Chuckles over here woke me up with no problem."

"You are the only one who has a problem. Lynne is okay."

Nate nudged me. "Yeah, but she's Mrs. Sunny."

"I wasn't aware she was married," I joked.

"Ms. Sunny then."

Kale looked at Nate and I, back and forth with disgust. "You two are morning people."

Nate and I both laughed. "Not especially," I said. "I just happened to be awake."

"And I'm an insomniac," Nate added in a matter-of-fact tone of voice. This time, it was both Kale and I staring at Nate. "What?" he said, shifting uncomfortably.

"Nothing."

"Absolutely nothing."

"You're an insomniac. So what?"

Kale and I rambled on for a few moments, until Nate stopped looking at us like we'd done something wrong. During the complete silence, Lynne walked into the kitchen and just stared at us.

I broke the awkward silence. "Well. Shall we move on?"

"Wait," Kale stopped me. "Did you check to see if the restrooms work?"

I looked around. "The downstairs is charred, and there is no upstairs bathroom."

"We could check next door," Lynne suggested.

We all agreed and decided this would be best.

The neighboring house was in great shape – except for the two rambling flesh-eaters that were just standing inside of it, appearing to be locked in. Since Kale was in front and he opened the door, he took them both out with his gun. We waited a few moments to see if any more came, but these appeared to be it.

"I call first shower!" Kale yelled and he took off down a long hallway that was on our right.

Lynne and I searched for another bathroom in the house but could not find one. By the time we had finished searching, Kale was already out of the shower.

"Man," we heard him telling Nate. "That water was super-hot. And I didn't have any soap. But it was worth it."

"I have soap," I told him.

He glanced in my direction and rolled his eyes. "Of course you do. Why didn't you tell me before I got into the shower?"

"If you hadn't taken off running, I would have given it to you."

Kale rolled his eyes again and stalked off in the direction of the living room.

"So," questioned Nate. "Who's next?" Lynne and I just looked at each other. "Me, then," he said. I handed him the bar of soap and he went to shower.

Lynne showered after her brother and I showered after her. By the time I got to shower, there was hardly any hot water left. But that didn't matter. It just felt good to be clean again. I could see the dirt and grime coming off of my body and when I got out and toweled off, I felt lighter. I bet that if I had weighed myself before and after the shower, I would have lost five pounds.

After our refreshing showers, we all packed up and headed out. Back to the road, to the highway – back to walking in a straight line for miles and miles. In all honesty, this life got boring sometimes. You know, aside from the jump scares from flesh-eaters time to time, but other than that…

We were running dangerously low on food. We had forgotten to stock up at the house where we showered and whatever we found on the highway diminished quickly. We were slowly starving to death, day by day.

That's the terrible thing about this world. The biggest threat were the zombies, I'll admit that. But even if you did survive the zombies, you'd have to deal with feeding yourself, and in my case, others. You couldn't get attacked by another wild animal, or I don't know, fall off a random cliff. You could avoid all of that, most likely. But you could also die from a random disease, like cancer or pneumonia. You could die from a bad heart, or bad kidneys.

Even if you avoided all of that, you would die in the end anyway. Your body would give up on you. You would cease. And what was the purpose of remaining alive in the first place?

I don't know the answer, and I have a feeling that I won't have the answer to it for quite some time.

We stopped walking after a few hours so that Kale could hunt for some game that might live in the nearby wooded area. Nate, Lynne and I sat in the small meadow-like area beside the road and waited for him, passing the time by just talking.

"Do you think that other countries are having the same problems as us?" Lynne asked.

I snorted. "Most of them, probably. And the ones that hate us are probably the ones who are immune and just refusing to help."

Nate disagreed. "No, it probably is the whole world. I mean, if a flesh-eater infused human gets on a plane and doesn't know that something is wrong…"

"How would you not know if something is wrong?" I asked him. "Oh yeah, Mark was nibbling on my arm affectionately, not because he was an undead monster. Puh-lease." I could tell my sarcasm was unappreciated by the glares that came from the pair. "What? It's true."

"It was just a thought," said Lynne, coming to the rescue of her brother, who then turned his glare on his own sister. I smirked at the anticipation of the sibling fight that was about to unfold.

"I can fight my own battles, Lynne," said Nate coldly.

"I was just trying to help."

"I don't need your help!"

"You do around her! You'll let her walk all over you, just because you think she's 'different'!" Nate looked like a fish gasping for breath, his gaping mouth fluttering open and closed. His cheeks were turning red, as I'm sure mine were. Lynne was breathing heavily and grinning evilly at her newfound strength over her brother. She had just made this awkward for everyone…

I decided to break through the awkwardness and silently congratulated myself for my bravery. "So…Lynne. Will you show me how to make…what's it called? A daisy chain?"

Lynne broke her glare at her brother and smiled at me. "Sure, Alex. Go pick some of these." She held up a white flower that had a bright green stem and a yellow center.

I rose quickly and hurried to the edge of the woods, trying to block out the conversation between Lynne and her brother. No doubt it had something to do with me. Curiosity got the best of me though and I started to eavesdrop on their argument. I heard a snippet of Nate's angry whisper.

"…say that in front of her?"

"She is not something to ogle at, Nathan!"

I snickered silently at the mention of Nate's full name. She must have been really pissed, or she just wanted to really piss him off.

"I know, I just…we can't be friends? I can't be friends with a girl? Besides, you don't have to fight my fights for me Lynne! I can handle myself."

"Not with her, obviously. You two won't end up as 'just friends,' especially not when you are trailing after her with hearts in your eyes like a lovesick puppy!"

"Just give her a chance, okay?" I heard Nate plead. I felt the blush burning my cheeks, and the smile forming on my lips. I liked being liked. It was a nice feeling, even if I wasn't going to act on it.

I gathered the rest of the "daisies" and sat next to Lynne, who taught me how to weave them together to form a long chain. At times I saw her glance over at Nate, whose cheeks were still red and was avoiding looking our way. She took the chain from me and tied it off with a complicated knot, then put it around my neck like a necklace.

"You look adorable!" she squealed and reached to her back pocket. When she found it empty, she chuckled. "I was going to take a picture but then realized that I no longer have a phone…"

I laughed too and put my arm around her. I held my arm out in front of us like there was a phone in my hand. "Make a face!" I told her, and she puckered her lips, while I stuck out my tongue. "Click!" I said, pretending to take a picture and show it to Lynne. "Isn't this one a good one?"

She laughed. "It's brilliant!"

"What's brilliant?" asked Kale, who was looking at me with a smirk. Probably laughing at me for having a daisy chain around my neck.

"Our picture!" I responded, jumping up. "Lynne taught me to make a daisy chain and I wanted to remember this moment forever, so we took a mental picture." Lynne giggled.

Kale just looked at me, scolding me with his eyes for being an immature little girl. I stuck my tongue out at him, and he cocked his head for emphasis. He put the bag that he was hauling over his shoulder on the ground. Inside were two rabbits, one squirrel, and a raccoon.

My stomach churned, both out of hunger and at the thought of eating a raccoon. But a badass had to eat, didn't she?

I built a fire while Kale skinned the animals and Nate and Lynne made a spit for the fire. It took Lynne and I a small while to come up with enough wood to keep the fire going and even longer to find kindling to start it. Even when the fire was going, it was dim and smoky from wet wood. It didn't give very much heat.

"Roamer at three-o-clock," called out Kale without even looking up from his skinning. I turned my head ninety-degrees and saw that there was a flesh-eater, just rambling about. You got those a lot in wooded and secluded areas. That's why we called them roamers. They roamed about, looking for the next meal without using their heightened sense of smell.

59

I sighed, pulled out my Glock, shot two rounds into the flesh-eater, and he went down. None of us bothered to check if he was dead again. In a place as quiet as this, we would be able to hear his grunts and groans and his shuffling feet trying to get back up underneath him.

I didn't even get up to shoot my gun.

Putting the gun down beside me, I looked over to Lynne who had her hands over her ears and a look of admiration on her face.

"What?" I asked her, after half a minute of her stares.

"You just...shot that thing without even standing and aiming..."

I snort. "It's thirty feet and a six-foot person. I am pretty sure any of you could do it too." Lynne shook her head and went back to drawing pictures in the dirt with a stick. I reclined back on my elbows, letting my hair free of my neck, feeling the warm sun on my pale face. Closing my eyes, I thought about tomorrow.

We wouldn't be camping there, since we'd already seen one flesh-eater. Though I supposed one of us could have kept watch. It was a decent enough place to sleep. There was thick grass and the sound of the night surrounding you. I sighed, anxious for the night.

I was still fantasizing about the cool, dark night when I felt a nudge on my shoulder. Opening my eyes, I turned my head to see Nate looking at me. That's when I realized the others had gone, and it was just the two of us. Why was I always left alone with this confusing and infuriating boy?

"What?" I asked him, using the same tone as I'd used with his sister not ten minutes ago. I remembered what his sister had said about him liking me and I had to keep my cheeks from burning by biting on their insides. He was looking at me expectantly, so perhaps he had asked me a question. "Did you say something?" I asked.

"I said, don't sell yourself short. It takes skill to hit a target in the bull's-eye without standing or aiming." He was cleaning his knives, taking a piece of cloth and running it down the blades. He had to take care not to rip the cloth, lest the blade be dulled. I watched the grimy metal turn to shining silver in a matter of seconds – the gray and brown hilts to black.

He saw me staring and offered me the rag, but I shook my head in return. I didn't care enough about my knives to clean them. I didn't use them enough anyway. I looked around and remembered our missing friends.

"Where are Lynne and Kale?" I asked him, my voice sounding sluggish and a bit uninterested.

He glanced up at me, his mouth turning up into a grin. "I don't quite know what Kale is doing, but he went in that direction." He pointed to the left and I nodded. "But Lynne said that she was going to the 'ladies room' and went off in the opposite direction…that was five minutes ago."

I furrowed my brow. "No screaming or shots heard?"

"None whatsoever," he replied with a smirk that confused me. What was so funny? "Why are you smirking?" I asked him.

He laughed. "I am imagining what I am going to do to those two if they are flirting or making out back there. I would send you to go find them, but I'm sure you wouldn't want to be traumatized by it. I know I don't want to go searching for those two."

I laughed too and rolled my eyes, pushing myself up from the ground. "I'll go get them," I drawled.

He grinned up at me. "Thanks Lex."

I immediately whipped around at the new nickname and stared at him pointedly. I absolutely *hated* it when people called me that, even before this disaster. My grandmamma used it when she teased me, and that is the name she used for me when I was a little girl.

"What? You don't like Lex?" he asked me.

I shook my head, hard. "It's too girly. I like my other nickname."

He looked confused. "Your other nickname? Wait, Alex isn't your full name?" I shook my head again and he shrugged. "Okay, then. Alex it stays. If you don't mind me asking, what is your full name? Alexis?"

"Absolutely not," I scoffed, a shudder intruding. Another name that I hated. "My full name was Alexandra Grason."

He still looked confused. "Was? Isn't it still?"

I shuddered again. "No. My name is Alex. It ends with that."

"Well, why? I mean, don't get me wrong, I like Alex, but what is wrong with Alexandra?"

"Just like the others. It's too girly. It's who I was. Not who I am."

"You weren't always hard-ass Alex?"

I laughed and sat down again. "I wish. No. I used to be girly, like your sister." I jerked my thumb over my shoulder in the direction of Lynne. "I used to be like her before all of this."

Nate stared at me with an odd expression. "I honestly couldn't imagine that," he finally said after a few moments. "I mean, unfriendly, tomboy, fighter Alex was a popular little girly girl? Even with that daisy thing around your neck I can't imagine it. No way."

I laughed. "You already have half of that wrong. I just said that I was girly. I never said that I was popular or well-liked."

"You were..." Nate's question was cut off by the return of Lynne and Kale. I smirked and turn to Nate, who had a disgusted expression on his face.

They were arguing animatedly, yet their whispers told Nate and I that they were up to no good together. In a second, his expression turned from disgusted to pained and I had to suppress a giggle. I just grinned instead.

"So..." I drawled, interrupting their hushed argument. "Kale. Where is the food? And why did you leave?"

He looked at me with a glare. "The food is right here." He pointed to his pack. "And I was looking for water while you two were sitting here having a good ol' time."

I shrugged. "Tell us where you are going and what you are doing next time and we would have no need to be suspicious. And why do you have the food? We could just camp here tonight."

"And I suppose you will take the watch?" he asked.

"Not all night. But I can take first watch, if one of you takes the second. In fact, why don't we all take part in watch tonight, hrmm?" Kale glared at me and I gave him an insincere smile. "Does that not sound fair?" I looked to Lynne, who seemed to be cowering under my stare. "Doesn't that sound great Lynne?"

She nodded her head slowly, and it took everything in me to keep from laughing. I had to bite my lip and keep a straight face, and that is nearly impossible.

"Why don't you get out our food, Kale?" Nate called out from behind me, and I turned to him, letting my devilish smile sneak through my composure. He grinned back evilly.

Kale sat with a roll of his eyes and got out the cooked rodents. He threw, what I assumed was a squirrel, my way and I started eating. Man, I was starving for a home cooked meal. Or at least, a meal that wasn't canned and cold.

Nate had a rabbit, as did Kale, while Lynne and I ate the raccoon together.

Those poor animals. They were gone within ten minutes' time. Not that I regret it; they were delicious.

The fire was dimming further, though it was already dim to begin with. I threw in the animal bones and a log, and we all settled in for the night.

Lynne set up her little bed right next to mine. She used her softened bag as a pillow, and fell asleep immediately. Kale usually set up his sleeping area away from the rest of us, and that is just what he did this time. He was sleeping twenty feet from the fire and Nate, Lynn, and me. Nate was the last to fall asleep. He was four feet from his sister, and maybe ten from me. His head was turned toward me and the clothes that he used as a pillow were tucked under his head, and so were his hands.

I sat down, staring at the fire for maybe three hours before I felt myself dozing off. Shaking myself out of it, I got up and stretched out my limbs. This just made me even drowsier when I sat back down. I was nodding off for about the third time when I felt a hand on my shoulder, which made me jump.

I turned quickly and saw that it was just Kale . He looked at me sympathetically, and pushed me gently toward my pack.

"Go get some sleep, Alex," he said softly. I nodded and laid my head down on my pillowcase full of clothes. I was out in five seconds.

Chapter 9

I woke to the smell of burning pine needles. Looking around with my tired, groggy eyes, I realized that everyone else was already fully awake, with the exception of Lynne, who looked as if she were about to fall over from exhaustion. She had probably been the last to take watch. It was day, probably eight or nine in the morning.

"Good morning," called over Nate.

I waved him off. I didn't have the patience for his morning cheeriness. Stretching out my tired limbs I got up and walked around. The source of the burning smell was just the fire. Somebody must have thrown some green pine branches over it, to extinguish it.

I yawned. It was mornings like this when I missed my AudioHolo. I used to sit by the window upstairs or on the patio, drinking either hot chocolate or coffee, and just listen to music. It was the perfect kind of day for that. It was about seventy degrees, and there was a slight breeze that ruffled my long hair.

I checked the bandage on my arm. The bullet wound was healing nicely, and didn't hurt as much anymore. I took this as signal to put on my flannel.

I got one arm in the sleeve without any problem but my right arm couldn't make it through with the bandage. So I unwrapped the sweater from around my arm and set it on the ground. I would still need it, seeing that if I moved too much, my arm would start bleeding again. But it would have to wait. I put my arm through, then pushed and rolled up the sleeve so that it was rolled up on my shoulder. Then, with difficulty, I rewrapped the wound.

"Here, let me help…" started Nate, but I cut him off with a grunt and a wave of my hand. I didn't need his help with everything. I was perfectly capable.

Once it was badly wrapped, I shrugged and let it go. I would have to re-dress it in something different sooner or later, but I didn't have anything clean. If I used the clothes from my bag or the clothes from one of my friends, it would likely become infected very quickly.

I took inventory of the items in my pack. Other than my weapons and ammunition, the only other things I had in the small bag were my pillowcase of clothing, one bag of the McDonald's crackers, an empty plastic water bottle, an empty refillable water bottle, and two packets of water-flavoring stuff.

Leaving the plastic water bottle on the ground, I put everything back except for one packet of water flavoring. I shook it, to make sure all of the powder was at the bottom of the pack, and ripped the top off. I put some on my finger and sucked it off. Mmm. Tasted like fruit punch.

I rolled the top of the pack and stood up to see the group staring at me, like usual. Man, I must have been a really strange person, if they were always staring at me like that.

"Did you just suck water flavoring off of your finger?" asked Lynne.

I nodded. "So?"

She shook her head. "You really shouldn't do that Alex. It isn't to be consumed when it isn't diluted by water."

Kale laughed at this. "Who cares? That stuff is sweet, right? And I have such a sweet tooth. Can I get some of that?" I nod and hand over the small packet.

He dumped some in his mouth, then handed it over to Nate, who did the same. Nate then passed it to his sister, who took it reluctantly. She dumped the remainder in her mouth, then puckered her lips and closed her eyes.

"What?" I question her. "It's just fruit punch..."

"I know, " she responded, opening her eyes and grimacing. "It was just really strong. Really *sweet*." We all had to hold back laughs as she continued to wince and pucker her lips from the sweet powder that remained in her mouth.

"Does anyone else think we should get moving?" asked Nate. "I mean, Alex just patched up her shoulder again, and it was still bleeding a bit. Won't the smell attract the flesh-eaters?"

I hadn't really considered this, though I supposed it made sense. We must have killed off all of them on the highway when I got shot, but there might have been some near us now. And before, I had cleaned the wound with acetone and the sharp stench of the ketone chemical masked the scent of my blood. But there, where there was just nature surrounding us, there was no mask. Flesh-eaters would probably be tailing us when we left.

"He's right," I spoke up, and they all moved to pack up camp. We were ready to go in no more than sixty seconds.

Kale's "Let's go," was drowned out by the wails of a flesh-eater that emerged through the trees. He shot it down and we hurried out of the woods.

We ended up back on the highway next to a pile-up of cars and a horde of flesh-eaters. Nate brought out what I am going to call mini-broadswords and impaled several of them on the sharp, silver blade. I pulled out my trusty Glock and began firing. Kale was already twisting and stabbing and shooting the zombies, and Lynne was still fumbling around for bullets for her shotgun.

The flesh-eaters were all on the ground in a matter of five minutes.

"Well," said Nate, wiping the sweat from his forehead. "That was fun, now wasn't it?" Kale chuckled and I smiled, while Lynne looked at me with a suspicious look. I so don't know what that was for, considering I hadn't done anything to her, but hey, who knew?

We walked. Like usual, we walked. We walked on and on and on. We walked so far that it made me want to throw up. Nope, that was just the smell of the summer apocalypse that made me gag. False alarm.

We walked along an exit until it dumped us on a one-way road that was in the middle of the woods. It was starting to get dark, so we needed to find a place to camp – preferably not the woods, where a flesh-eater could happen upon you at any moment.

"Guys," I pointed out. "A driveway." It was, too. It had a large, ornate, white mailbox in front of the black tar pavement. I could tell they were all just as excited as me to not have to sleep in the open again. Especially Lynne. She would probably have been jumping up and down giddily if she hadn't been exhausted.

Walking down that driveway took forever. It had to be a mile long. We were about to give up and turn around to find somewhere else when a house came into view.

"House" is not an appropriate word for this gargantuan mansion. It was at least four stories, with two balconies on each upper floor. We all looked on at the dark-red brick and white trim in awe. It seemed to be in great shape, no flesh-eaters around or anything. I could see the backup generators, and hear them thrum with electricity. Where did they get their power? I then saw the huge windmill and solar panels that ran along the roof of the mansion.

We all walked toward the house, using the stone path that was flanked by flowers on either side. These were dead, but the ivy clinging to the sides of the brick was still alive and well. I felt a drop of water plop onto my skin and looked up. The sky was cloudy and gray and I could practically see the rain falling toward us.

"Let's get inside," I said, and they all looked up and nodded. We hurried to the front door and prayed that it was unlocked.

No such luck.

"Screw this!" Kale shouted, and shot the lock with his gun. He shoved the door open and waved a hand inside. "Entre vous," he said and we all stepped in.

The foyer of this house was bigger than my living room back home. It had large marble stairs that led up to the upper floors and an elevator over in the corner. It was decorated with large, beautiful paintings and great glass sculptures.

We all split up and searched the house, starting on the first floor and working our way up to the top. No flesh-eaters anywhere. I found this strange. This place had to have had maids or servants or something. There was no way anyone would stay in this house without help.

I was still admiring the ginormous bathtub on the third floor when I heard Lynne scream. I ran out of the bathroom, and looked around. It sounded like it was coming from the top floor. I met Nate at the stairs and we took them two at a time.

The top floor consisted of a huge loft, a large bedroom and a bathroom that was almost the same size as the kitchen. We found Lynne in the bedroom, staring into a set of double doors. Her mouth was hanging open and she was still staring.

Kale arrived in the room a moment later. "What happened?" he asked her worriedly. She shook her head, her mouth still gaping.

I held my gun high. "Let's take a look, shall we?" I opened the doors, and was immediately shocked just as much as Lynne. Inside was a huge walk-in closet. There were racks and stacks of clothing on both sides of the walls, and shoes lining the back wall. There was men's clothing on the left side, and women's on the right. We all walked in and just turned around in awe. A small crystal chandelier hung from the ceiling.

Kale turned to Lynne. "This is why you screamed? Clothes?" He was still staring at her with a look of wonder. "Why?"

I looked at him and laughed. "You have got to be kidding me. She's a girl. She loves clothes. And I have to admit, I am pretty excited to see this too. New, fabulous clothes!" I giggled with Lynne and both boys stared at me. They had never seen me so girly and excited. The only thing they had ever seen was rough-edged, tough, I-don't-take-any-bull-from-anyone Alex. It was just then that they got to see a glimpse of whom I used to be.

Lynne ran into the closet and started stripping eagerly. "Whoa, whoa there girly. Hold on a sec." I shut the doors behind us and she changed into the first dress she touched, which happened to be a long, sparkly gown. She picked out a pair of heels and put them on too then checked out her new outfit in a nearby, floor-length mirror. It was a bit big on her but it suited her looks well.

She opened the door and showed the boys, taking a few poses as Nate pretended to be paparazzi and I stifled a laugh. I pushed Lynne back into the closet. "Try a few more!" I shouted through the closed doors. Kale rolled his eyes and headed downstairs. Perhaps he was getting something to eat. I was hungry but that could wait. I could have a little more fun before getting back to depressing survival.

Nate and I parked our butts on a soft couch that was in the corner of the room, facing the closet. He sat like he was at home already, with his ankle propped up on his knee and one arm draped over the back of the couch. I sat Indian-style, or 'crisscross-applesauce' we called it when we were young.

Lynne emerged dressed in a ridiculous black dress. It looked like somebody had draped a curtain over her shoulder and called it a dress. She wore the same black heels as with the other dress.

Nate laughed. "That thing is ridiculous. What would anyone wear a curtain to?"

Lynne blushed and smiled. "It was in a bag that said 'Funeral.'" She laughed with Nate, and I smiled.

"You should try something on, Alex," Kale suggested from across the room. I hadn't even noticed his return. There was a devious look in his eye and a smirk on his face.

"No, I don't..." I tried protesting but Lynne grabbed me by the arm and dragged me into the closet.

"Yeah, it's so much fun, Alex!" Lynne closed the door behind her and threw a small, black, white and red dress at me. "Put this one on!"

I chuckled. "Oh, all right," I said, and unzipped the dress. I slid into the short-sleeved dress with ease. It came down to my knees, and was a little tight around them, though I think it was made that way. I looked into the mirror and laugh. I looked like a reporter from the 1930s. I saw a pair of white, elbow-length gloves and put them on with the dress, with a large white and black hat and a pair of sunglasses. Not too long ago, this look would have been in style. The old-time look came back in only 100 years after it had left.

Lynne turned around in a sundress and gasped at my accessorizing. "You look awesome!" she squealed and handed me a pair of red heels to put on with it. I looked at them dubiously then slipped out of my combat boots. I hadn't worn anything but those for a few months. It felt weird to be wearing heels again.

"Can you zip it?" I asked her, and she nodded with excitement. She could barely contain herself. "Jeez, Lynne," I said to her. "It's just a dress."

"I know," she squealed, "but you look amazing!"

"Thank you, darling," I drawled out in a snooty voice.

She smirked and put her arm through mine, our hands on our hips. We opened the door and stepped out. Kale and Nate stared at the two of us, who were posing and blowing kisses to each other, giggling like schoolgirls.

Kale whistled, and started to laugh. "Wow," he said. "Alex, in a dress? And those accessories…" He continued to laugh.

"And she picked them all out herself!" Lynne added proudly.

I blushed and looked away from them. I used to read all the fashion magazines before. I knew a thing or two about accessories. Of course, they didn't need to know that.

"You both look great," Nate said, and Lynne and I laughed.

"Thank you, darling," I repeated the drawl. We all started goofing around, until Lynne and I both pushed Nate into the closet and forced him to change into one of the outfits.

"Pick a good one!" Lynne called to him through the door. "Nothing that makes you look stupid! You know what, I'm coming in there!"

"What! No!" Nate's muffled voice yelled at her through the door. I looked away when she opened one of the doors and slipped inside. I heard them shuffle around, and a groan before Nate walked out a few moments later, in an outfit to match mine. He was wearing a suit with a bowtie and a fedora.

"Perfect!" Lynne shouted when she came back out. "Now you two could be going to a dinner in the nineteen-thirties, or something."

I laughed and Nate blushed. He held out his arm to me. "My lady?"

"Oh, well of course, sir!" I said, and took it. We walked around like this for a few moments until everyone broke down in laughter, including Kale.

"Hey Kale," I said to him, eyes still watering. "You should find an outfit to match Lynne's."

He went wide-eyed, then laughed. "How about no?"

Lynne and I looked to each other, plotting against him until we heard a loud but muffled scream. We looked out the windows into the rainstorm, to see a handful of flesh-eaters attacking a man on the front lawn.

CHAPTER 10

"We have to help him," I yelled to them, and they all nodded in agreement. I grabbed the Glocks from my bag and took a knife when I realized that I was still in a dress and heels with nowhere to store the knife. I dropped it and kicked off the heels, running full speed towards the stairs. Or, it would have been full speed if the dress hadn't been slowing me down. I had to stop and rip the dress down the seam so that I would have full leg use.

I got outside and the wind and storm tore the hat off of my head. The cold rain splattered onto my exposed skin, making me shudder. The man was on the ground not forty feet away but he wasn't moving. The flesh-eaters were moving in quickly. I raised my gun and shot two of them in the legs, hobbling them, but it wasn't enough. The others circled around him and I tried to shoot them all as I ran towards him.

His ear-piercing, blood-curdling screams as the zombies tore into his flesh filled the air, and by then I knew it was too late. Now the others were around me, helping me take the other flesh-eaters down, taking our time. It was far too late for this man. He would die soon, the infected blood would course through his system quickly. If not today, then he would become a flesh-eater by tomorrow morning.

We took them down one by one, in minutes, and surrounded the man who was writhing in agony. We tried to calm him down but he was in too much pain. I didn't even know if he could see us.

"Sir?" Lynne squeaked out. "Sir, can you hear us?"

"It's no use, Lynne," Kale sighed. "He won't make it."

I nodded to him, looked down at the man, and sighed. "I am really sorry, sir," I said, and I shot him in the face.

He went slack immediately and hot bile rose in the back of my throat. He had been still alive but he'd been bitten. He was going to die anyway, then come back to life – as a blood-thirsty monster. So I guess I'd been saving my friends and myself?

I saw a gleam on the ground next to him, and I looked to see what it was.

It was a key. Presumably, the key to the house. The house had been locked when we came, and Kale shot the lock out...then barricaded it. We locked this man out of his own home, and he died because of it. I felt light-headed. I killed this man on his own lawn.

"Let's go inside," Kale says, and I from the corner of my eye I saw him taking my expression in.

We sat around the island in the middle of the large kitchen. All of the stuff in the fridge was no longer any good to us, being at least a few months old, so we had to raid the even larger pantry. That guy must have been loaded. I mean, we could have told you that just by looking at the house, but his whole pantry was stocked. Chips, cookies, peanut butter, jelly, crackers and....

"Is that..." I started to ask, before Lynne shoved me aside and grabbed for it.

"Chocolate! Oh, sweet chocolate!" She hugged a candy bar to her chest and started kissing it. "Oh, I missed you soo much chocolate!"

"Long distance relationship?" Kale asked from behind, and the others laughed, despite what they just witnessed, and what I'd just done.

"Oh my god, you have no idea."

There was enough for all of us and I took up a bar and examined the faded label. It said "Hershey's Milk Chocolate Bar." I ripped open the foil wrapper, shoved half of the chocolate bar into my mouth and let it melt on my tongue. And then I thought of the key in that man's hand and it turned to ashes in my mouth.

"It is soooo good!" Lynn moaned loudly, and Kale mumbled out a yes in agreement.

The only one of us who hadn't stuffed his face with chocolate was Nate. He was holding his and staring at it before putting it back in the pantry. He saw me staring and shrugged. I offered him the rest of my chocolate bar and he shook his head. "I don't like chocolate," he explained, and I raised my eyebrows. I set my chocolate bar on the counter and tried not to look at it.

We started looking for real food to make and came up with an unopened box of macaroni and cheese. There were three boxes, so we made two and saved the other for another time.

We stuffed ourselves full, and drank the unopened water bottles that we found on the floor of the pantry.

Lynne and Nate went to go take showers in their respective rooms while Kale and I continued to raid the pantry. We were looking for soda when Kale came across a box of wine. He picked it up and looked at it, then spotted more alcohol behind it. This guy had bottles of vodka, liquor, rum, beer, and those lemonade-alcohol mixed-drink things. Kale was about to pop the lid off the liquor when I stopped him.

"What are you doing?" I asked him.

"You have got to be kidding me. Has goody-two-shoes over here never had any alcohol?"

I winced. "I had wine at a wedding once but other than that, no I have not."

He snickered. "I figured." He broke the seal and took a sip. He sighed, and I swiped the bottle from him. "What are you doing, Blondie?" he asked, aggravating me further.

"We are in the middle of a zombie apocalypse," I growled, "and you want to get drunk? You could die out there."

He made a face. "It's just liquor. If you don't want to get drunk, then go drink one of those fruity little drinks over there." He pointed to the alcohol-infused lemonade and grabbed the bottle from me. He took another slug and smiled.

"I won't be drinking at all, thank you," I told him. "I take protecting my friends' lives and my own seriously, unlike you, apparently."

He scowled at me. "I protect them just as much as you do!" He took another sip and I threw my hands up. I wouldn't keep him from making terrible decisions. He would just have to realize that tomorrow. And when he was throwing up in the bathrooms upstairs, I wouldn't be the one to hold his hair back.

I stomped off to my room on the third floor and ran into Nate, who still had beads of water in his hair. He was in a change of clothes—a long sleeved blue T-shirt with a regular pair of blue jeans and a pair of sneakers.

"Whoa, what's up?" he asked me. "You look pissed."

I snarled in disgust. "Kale is getting drunk."

Nate's eyes flashed. "Is he crazy? What if we get attacked? He'll get killed!"

"Go tell him that," I snorted. "I'm going to take a shower. If you need me to whup his ass, just come in and holler."

He nodded and rushes down the stairs to confront Kale while I headed to my room and checked it out. I chose the one closest to Lynne's, which was just across the hall. Nate's was down the hall and across from Kale's room. My room was a dark blue, with a large, four-poster bed in the middle. The covers were purple and white, with matching drapes. There was a MacroHolo in the middle of the wall farthest from the bed.

Apparently, there was a walk-in closet in every room, because I had one in my room too. It wasn't nearly as large as the other one but this one was still bigger than my room back home.

I grabbed a new pair of skinny jeans, a white tank top and a plaid, yellow, purple, and gray flannel. I kept my combat boots. There was no way I was leaving those there. I also grabbed underwear and a bra, then headed into the bathroom.

The showerhead had five different settings. There were five different types of shampoo alone. A small, round, pink puffball hung from the faucet. I jumped into the shower and sighed. I hadn't even realized I was cold until I jumped into the hot shower. Of the five shampoos, I chose a coconut lime that smelled like the tropics. I scrubbed it into my long hair, using my nails to get to my scalp. Then I used the body wash and conditioner of the same scent.

The hot water and soap made my bullet-graze sting like crazy, but now it was clean, at least. I stepped out of the shower, dried off, and got dressed. I left the flannel off until I could find proper bandages, which had to be somewhere in this enormous house. Checking in the drawers and cabinets of the bathroom, I came across a sealed plastic package of gauze. Bingo.

I took the package and went to look for somebody to wrap my arm, deciding to start in the kitchen, because Nate and Kale might still be quarreling. One step into the kitchen caused me to wrinkle my nose. It reeked of spirits, but nobody was in there so I looked elsewhere. Kale was on the couch snoring—fast asleep. I wasn't surprised. I knew for a fact that Lynne was still in the shower when I left my room because I could hear her water running. I decided that Nate must be in his room so I walked up the two flights of stairs and knocked on the door.

"Come in," I heard Nate say, sounding aggravated. I opened the door and stepped inside onto the lush gray carpet. Nate's room was a deep red, with accents of grays and black. His bed was the same as mine—a large four-poster—but his covers were black and gray instead of purple. He was sitting in a chair by a window, engrossed in the book in his hand.

"What's up?" I asked him, leaning up against the door frame.

He glanced up at me and puts a bookmark in his book, placing it back on the bookshelf adjacent to the chair. "Just looking."

"I see you chose the only room with books," I said, smirking.

He smiled. "You can come in and look," he said.

I stepped farther inside and looked at the books on the small bookshelf. The entire top shelf was filled with a series of books called "Harry Potter." I laughed and picked up a heavy blue one. "I read this series before," I said, laughing. I had found it ridiculous, yet funny and I never put it down.

"I have, too," he laughed, taking the book from my hands. "This one was my favorite, because of the evil hag whose name I can't remember."

"Umbridge," I stated, and he nodded. We stood in a comfortable silence for a moment before Nate asked me if I needed anything.

"Oh, I need you to wrap my arm again," I told him. He nodded and motioned for me to sit on the bed. I sat, sinking down a few inches on the soft comforter. I handed him the bandages and he opened the pack.

"Did you clean it well?" he asked me. I grimaced and nod, and he chuckled. "Yes, I bet it hurt. But I guess it was worth it now since it is clean and smells like coconuts."

I narrowed my eyes. Was he flirting with me? Oh, I so don't do flirting. "Yeah," I answered. "It stung like crazy though."

"I can imagine," he said softly, concentrated on wrapping my arm. When he ran out of bandage, he held his hand out to me and I just looked at him. "Give me the tape," he replied to my confused look.

I shook my head. "I didn't see or bring any tape."

"Then I'm going to just tuck the end into the bandage. I am really sorry if this hurts," he said. He took the end and shoved it into the top of the bandage, his fingers grazing the wound a bit. It hurt, but I just grimaced and waited. "All done," he said finally and I stood up.

"Thank you," I said to him, and he nodded.

"You're welcome. And if you want to borrow a book, you can."

"I'm beat. I'm going to sleep. Oh, that reminds me. Why does the kitchen smell like alcohol so bad?"

Nate grimaced. "I was arguing with Kale about drinking and he was fighting me for the bottle. It shattered and went all over the floor. He started complaining and carrying on until I told him to go to bed. Is he still on the couch?"

"Yeah," I told him. "Did you get it cleaned up?"

"Yeah. I also dumped the rest of the alcohol down the drain. I have no idea if there is more somewhere, but we better keep an eye out."

"That's for sure." I nodded. "Well, thanks again." I turned my back to him and walked into the hallway. I was just turning the knob to get into my own room when I heard Nate call out to me.

"Wait!" he called, and ran down to my room. "I forgot that I wanted to ask you something."

I just waited for him to ask me and he continued when he realized that he wasn't going to get a response. "Why did you bleach your hair blonde?" he asked me, and I smirked. He must have been wondering that ever since he'd talked to Lynne about how it was "different."

"I didn't." He gave me a puzzled look, and I sighed. "I was born with blonde hair," I explained.

"How?" he asked me.

I told him about how both of my parents were heterozygous and his eyes got glassy. I chuckled.

"But what about your eyes?" he asked.

"Born with it."

"That is so cool," he told me.

I snorted. "Glad you think so."

"Do you mean people always made fun of you and stuff?"

"Yeah," I answered him. He thought this over, and I sighed once more. "I'm going to sleep," I told him. "Goodnight, Nate." I walked in to my room without a backward glance, shutting the door behind me.

CHAPTER 11

The next morning I woke up in a comfortable bed with a large comforter thrown over me. I sighed, wishing it were like this all the time. I got up and stretched before heading into the bathroom to inspect myself in the mirror where I had to blink twice before I realized that the person staring back at me was actually me.

I had a minor cut under my eye, and a yellowing bruise under that. There was a white scar just above my upper lip and another near my hairline. My face was slim and I guessed my body was too. My rat's nest that I call hair came down to my waist, and was lighter than I remembered it ever being. I was tan, though not too tan, like Kale. I'm probably just noticing these things because I'm looking for them. Or, more like, looking for the person I used to be.

"What happened to me?" I asked myself. Oh, right. The apocalypse. Now I remembered. I dug through the drawers, looking for a suitable brush for my hair, and came up with a light-pink one with different size bristles. I attacked the giant knots until my hair was smooth. Now that all the knots were gone, I realized that my hair actually came down to the middle of my forearms. My bangs had grown out and were hanging in my eyes. I didn't bother with them.

I exited the bathroom, turning off the light on the way. I was about to get my Glocks out of my bag until I realized that I'd left them in the kitchen, and my bag upstairs. A thought clicked into my head. Maybe I could find a suitable bag for all of my stuff in the major closet upstairs, if I couldn't find one in here.

I searched my closet and came up with nothing, so I headed upstairs where I found a black book bag that should suit my needs. I shoved everything into my new bag, including my Glocks and knives. Then I left my bag in my room and headed into the kitchen, where Lynne and Nate sat at the counter, deep in discussion. I decided not to interrupt just yet and waited just outside the archway.

I know, I know. I tended to eavesdrop. But, I couldn't help it. I was a curious person.

"Nate, no. I told you no."

"Why?" Nate asked, desperation in his voice.

"You will get far too attached."

Attached to what?

"Then why don't you let Alex decide?" he asked. "I'll go wake her now."

I heard a creak as he got up from his chair and my eyes widened as I realized that I was about to be caught eavesdropping. But Nate didn't exit, so I become confused. Then I heard another creak and realized that Lynne had just pulled him back into his chair.

"No, Nate. She needs to rest."

"She can go back to sleep after I ask her if we can stay here."

I sighed. He wanted to stay in the house. There was absolutely no way we were staying there. It might have been nice, but we wanted to get to Shenandoah as soon as possible. Plus, the woods around us didn't have much food. And our stock would run out eventually.

"What makes you think she will want to stay here? She killed a man on the front lawn, and you can't pretend that you didn't see the grief on her face after. Just wait till she comes downstairs." Lynne told him.

That was enough of that conversation. "Wait till I come downstairs for what?" I asked them, entering the room.

"Oh, nothing," Nate responded sheepishly. I raised an eyebrow.

Lynne sighed. "He wants to stay in the mansion."

"Oh, absolutely not," I told him, pretending as if the idea had never crossed my mind. Believe me, it had. But there were far too many cons.

His face fell and I felt bad. So I explained my thoughts and he nodded, though I could tell that he still wanted to stay. I understood, even if I didn't agree. This place was nice.

"We had better wake Kale up," I told them.

"Kale was already awake," Lynne said. "He woke up and had a massive headache. So we gave him some Advil and he passed out again."

I sighed. He had a hangover. "Well, Nate," I said. "It must be your lucky day. We get to stay another day until Kale sleeps off his hangover." Nate's grin was broad and it made me give a small smile.

We went through the day pilfering the house of its nonperishable goods, including food and medical supplies. We all took another set of fresh clothes, too. Among the things I took were more peanut butter, beef jerky, the box of mac and cheese, two plastic packs of bandages, Band-Aids, and two bottles of water, both refillable.

Lynne took some dried fruit, along with another two sets of clothes and prescription meds. Nate took more nonperishable foods, some eating utensils, and a really cool collapsible pot. Kale didn't even bother helping. He apparently had the worst headache I'd ever seen. He locked himself in his room and didn't come out at all, except to eat a bit of fruit.

By the time we were done gathering everything we both needed and wanted, it was night again. We all said our goodnights and went to our rooms to get a good night's sleep for tomorrow's day of traveling.

I usually didn't dream when I slept. Well, I guess I did, since it's proven that you always dream, but I usually don't remember them. Not that night. I remember my dream clearly. Though it was more of a nightmare.

I was sitting in the pantry of the house, reading a book. It was *Harry Potter and the Order of the Phoenix*. I had just started when somebody came into the pantry. It was pretty dark, so I couldn't see his face. He came in and started talking to me. "Who are you?" he asked me. "What are you doing in here?" I told him I was reading and he replied that it was too dark to read. So he flipped a switch next to the door, and I saw his face. He was the man from the front lawn. And we weren't in the pantry anymore. We were in the large, walk-in closet from the top floor. And I was wearing the dress that Lynne had made me try on, with all of the accessories and even the heels.

"Why did you kill me?" he asked me. I tried to tell him that it was because he was turning into a zombie, but my voice wouldn't work. "Why would you kill an innocent man who had no intentions of hurting you?"

"Flesh-eaters," I choked out, and he shook his head.

"No. I wasn't one. I wasn't going to become one. But you are." I shook my head vigorously and started running. But I couldn't run fast enough because the dress was too tight. So I stopped to try and rip it, but it wouldn't rip. Not even along the seams. The man caught up to me and pushed me over. I tried to grab onto something, but there was nothing. We were in a dark hallway, and there was nowhere to run to. He grabbed me by the wrist and I screamed, thinking that death was in my immediate future.

CHAPTER 12

"Alex! Alex! Wake up!" Nate was shaking me. I opened my eyes and blinked. The light was on in my room, and Lynne and Nate were staring at me with concern. "Are you okay?" Nate asked.

I rubbed my eyes and sat up. "What time is it?" I looked at the clock and saw that it was only 1:47 in the morning. I looked at them again. "Why are you in my room?"

Nate furrowed his brow, and Lynne looked at me in surprise. "You were screaming your head off," she answered. "We came in here and tried to wake you up. It took us like five minutes to get you to wake up and stop screaming."

"I had a nightmare," I told them sheepishly. I smacked my lips together. My mouth was dry. "Lynne, can you get me a glass of water?"

"Of course," she said, and hurried out the door. Nate sat down next to me on the bed, running his hand over the comforter.

"It was that guy," I told him. He grimaced and looked away from me awkwardly. "He was chasing me. He tried to turn me. I couldn't run fast enough."

"I'm sorry it scared you," he said.

I winced. "It doesn't scare me," I told him coldly. "I feel guilty."

"Sorry," he said. "I didn't realize that it would weigh you down with that much guilt."

I laughed. "Just because I look like a hard-ass doesn't mean I like killing innocent people." He shifted uncomfortably. "Do you ever wonder if these flesh-eaters, these people, ever had family? Or a job, or something to live for?"

Nate shook his head.

"Well, I do," I told him. "All of the time. And killing somebody that was still alive, but bitten? That makes me feel like an awful person."

"But you just didn't want him to become a zombie," he reasoned with me. "You just wanted him to die as himself, not a bloodthirsty monster." I nodded, and he took my hand. "You are a good person, Alex. It didn't take me very long to see that."

I smiled at him, and Lynne walked back into the room with my water. Nate released my hand, for which I was grateful. I really didn't want his sister to suspect anything.

"I got you bottled water, because I heard that if you drink tap water before bed that you won't be able to sleep again."

I highly doubted that but I accepted the water and thanked her anyway. They told me good night, and shut the light out before closing the door. I took a sip of the water and put it on the nightstand before snuggling back into the blankets again. I thought about what Nate had said – that he thought that I was a good person, and I reflected on what he meant. Maybe he was referring to the lecture I'd given Kale after we first met each other. A small smile slid its way onto my face before I fell into a deep sleep.

CHAPTER 13

We all packed up and headed out at dawn. Kale was considerably better than he'd been the day before, thank goodness. I didn't think I could have stood it if he were constantly whining and carrying on about his headache. I hoped he'd learned his lesson.

We left the mansion and I think I was the only one who didn't look back at least once. I was sure they were going to miss that place, but I sure wouldn't. Bad memories. Terrible nightmares.

We continued on the highway we'd first come from. I had a knife and a Glock tucked into my waistband, and my other knife and Glock in the mesh side pockets of the book bag on my back.

Walking throughout the day and three hours into the night, we had a hard time finding a good place to fall asleep. Finally we found a pile-up of cars, and we rested there; two people to a car. I slept with Lynne in a minivan, while Nate slept in an SUV to our left and Kale kept watch. He woke Lynne up at three a.m. and she took the watch while he slept.

We switched guard position every night, and we continued like this for a whole week. In total, we probably killed around 250 flesh-eaters. Some days there were as many as fifty. Some, there were as few as five or six. We killed every one that crossed our path. This went well, until a flesh-eater horde snuck up on us.

It was Lynne's turn to take first watch, and we all settled into bed and fell asleep quickly, with no problems. I was dreaming about home-cooked food when I heard a loud scream that woke me from my dream. Sitting up, I grabbed my Glock, which I always kept beside me when I slept. Still half asleep, I looked for the trouble. I saw Lynne pointing, and Kale loading bullets into his shotgun.

"What is it?" I asked him groggily,

"A horde. Probably fifty of them? They took Lynne off of her guard."

I sighed. Of course. Lynne's turn to take watch, and we encountered a horde. "Well is everybody ready?" I asked them. Kale sighed, and Nate nodded his head sleepily. Lynne just stared. "Then let's do this," I said, a slight yawn interceding.

Kale took the left, Nate took the middle, and I took the right. Lynne, well, let's call her our "back-up." We whirled and stabbed and shot and killed until all of the flesh-eaters were lying on the ground at our feet. It took about ten minutes.

"You guys are amazing," Lynne said, and I shrugged. It wasn't that amazing…but okay. Whatever she said. I wasn't going to deny a compliment. I was so short on them, those days.

"Well, I'm not falling back to sleep," said Nate, and we all nodded. There was no sleeping after a fight like that. It just got your adrenaline going.

"Let's just walk. We can go faster if we just keep walking." Kale had a point.

So we walked. And walked. And walked. We walked through the day, and into the evening. We took three breaks. One for breakfast, another for a snack, and another for dinner.

We were all exhausted by the time the road had turned to dirt, and so happy too. We were in the country. In the country, it felt like we could be normal people, on an evening walk. It even smelled normal. Almost.

The sun was sinking below the horizon and the moon was making an appearance in the sky. You could actually see the stars that night, too. My grandmamma told me that when she was young, you could see the stars in the sky almost every night. But that was before the Earth was so polluted that you could barely breathe without the help of an oxygen mask.

The sky looked like Van Gogh's "Starry Night." It was twenty different shades of blue, and the stars were yellow and white flowers, opening their petals to us in the dark of the dusk. I didn't think my comrades looked at the sky and thought about the past like I did. Believe me, I was a "live in the present" kind of person, but when the present sucked, I thought I'd rather live in the past.

I looked at my friends, and wondered about their pasts. Really, I didn't know my friends' pasts. I knew their personalities – what they liked, what they hated, but I didn't know anything about them. I didn't know where they lived, or where they went to school—I didn't know if they had any other family. All I knew was what I had witnessed in the time I had spent with them.

Kale was leading us forward, like the strong man he was. I knew that he'd gone to a military-based school, but that was it. I remembered him telling me that he had a brother he was close to, but couldn't imagine any adults being very special to him. Otherwise, he would have been softer, and easier to understand.

Lynne trailed behind him like a lost puppy, looking at her nails, the ground, the sky, the trees, and the barn in the distance. I could see her sitting in her room with her friends, gossiping about so-and-so, who did whatever. I could imagine her being a person who was closer to her friends than her parents, and as someone who spent a lot of time outdoors.

Lastly, I looked to Nate. He was walking beside me, yet staring straight ahead, his gray eyes trained on the horizon. He didn't realize that I was staring at him, and analyzing his every move, watching his hair drift across his face and moving in different directions with every step. I could see him being alone. Being disliked. Being close to nobody, except for the person that he lived with, perhaps. Being like me.

I was still staring at Nate when suddenly, Lynne stopped walking. Nate and I stopped, because she was in front of us, but Kale kept walking, unaware that he was leaving his group behind.

"Kale!" I called out to him. "Wait, come back."

He turned around, saw that we had stopped moving, and then jogged back to us. "What?" he questioned Lynn. "What is it?"

"I thought I saw... a light...?" She pointed to the barn. "Over there. It was really faint and small, but...! There it is again, but closer and to the left!"

We all stared in the direction she was pointing, until Nate started laughing. "Lynne," he said. "That's a firefly."

"A firefly?" she asked. He nodded. Then she squealed, making me jump, and she ran off in the direction of the firefly.

"What are you doing?!" I called out to her.

"Catching fireflies!" I heard her respond. In other words, being a kid again. I looked at Kale, and he shook his head. Then I looked at Nate and he grinned.

"You want to?" he asked me. I laughed and ran out into the field as an answer.

By now, the fireflies had really come out, and the sun was nowhere to be seen. The small bugs twinkled like stars in the tall grass, and they were everywhere. One was shining right beside me. I lunged out and grabbed the glowing insect, and I felt it crawling around on my skin, tickling me. A giggle escaped from my mouth.

I looked over to Nate, who must have been watching a firefly somewhere near me, because he was looking in my direction – almost right at me. Checking my cupped hand, I found that the firefly had escaped, and I ran to catch another.

With a firefly in my grasp, I ran towards Lynne. She had captured two fireflies and had put them in an old oil lantern that Kale found in the barn. I saw her watching them float around and try to escape. Focusing more on getting there than on what lay in front of me, I wasn't quite watching where I was going.

So when I stumbled and fell, I was expecting it to just be a hole, you know?

I fell and squashed the bug in my hand. "Aweeee!" I cried, laughing. It wasn't until I tried to get up that I realized that what I tripped over wasn't a hole.

It was a hand.

I screamed and kicked at the flesh-eater's face, using my own booted feet as a weapon. I groped at my hip for my gun, pulled it, and shot. The flesh-eater's hand fell away and I was breathing heavy, a thin layer of sweat beading on my face. I put down my gun, wiped it away and picked up my gun again.

Nate, Lynne and Kale rushed over to me.

"Oh my God, are you okay?"

"I didn't see it until it was too late!"

"Good job handling yourself out there."

You can probably guess who said what on your own.

"Guys," I interrupted their babbling. "I'm okay. I got it." They all stared at me.

"O-okay," said Lynne. She turned away and started catching fireflies again. Kale went back to where he'd been sitting, on the steps to a back door of the barn.

Nate stayed though, and a worried look remained on his face. "Are you sure you're okay?" he asked.

I nodded and grinned, eager to get the questioning over with. I'd been having fun until that flesh-eater had grabbed my foot, and I was not letting it ruin it. Spotting a firefly near Nate's face, I grabbed it and squished it in my hands. I kept my hands in a circle, like a cage for the firefly, so that Nate thought that I still had it in my hand.

"Okay, then," he said and turned away. As soon as his back was to me, I wiped the firefly guts on his black T-shirt, smearing the glowing juices over the fabric. He turned around. "What was that?" he asked me. I grinned wider and put my palms up in an innocent, 'I don't know' expression. His eyes narrowed and the corners of his mouth turned up into a smile when he spotted my glowing hands.

I turned on my heel and ran away from him, knowing that he was going to chase after me with firefly guts on his own hands. Grabbing fireflies out of the air, I collected three or four in my hands at once and squished them together. Then I stopped running and looked for Nate.

He was nowhere to be found. I waited a moment, thinking that he was playing a joke. I was starting to get worried when I felt two hands cover my eyes from behind. "Guess who?" I heard Nate's voice, light with laughter. I laughed, and reached my hands behind my back to wipe the fireflies on the front of his shirt. He pulled his hands away immediately, and I opened my eyes.

It looked like everything was glowing a yellowish-green. I looked at Nate to see that he was examining the damage on his only shirt.

"You have a little something on your shirt," I pointed out, my voice serious.

"Actually, it's a lot of something," he laughed.

"Guys!" Lynne called out. "We had better get some shelter. It's getting late. And I think it might rain!"

"Good idea," I yelled back. "How about the barn?"

"Sounds good."

We all grabbed our packs and headed in the direction of the barn. Kale was inside first, obviously, and it seemed like he had found a source of light for us to eat and wash up by. Nate and I walked side-by-side to the barn, still laughing and making jokes about fading stains on our shirts.

The barn was dusty and smelled like barnyard animals and musk. Kale and Lynne dropped their packs on the floor beside a sawhorse and a wheelbarrow. The light that I'd seen from outside came from a small oil lamp that flickered and smelled funny.

"I don't know how good the oil is in this," Kale explained when he saw the sour look on my face. "I think that's why it smells weird."

Lynne glanced at me, and then did a double-take. She laughed and looked over at Nate. "Did you two have a war?"

"Yes," I answered. "We are mortal enemies in the War of the Fireflies. Why do you ask?"

She laughed and Nate and I started our search for a water source to clean off our firefly stains. We finally found a gray, rusty sink near the back of the barn that was hidden by large piles of rotting hay. We used one of Lynne's five extra shirts and tore it into two to wipe ourselves off.

I did the best I could for my face without a mirror, and Nate got everything on his front. But he was having trouble seeing the faded guts on the back of his shirt.

"Turn around," I told him. "I'll get it." He obeyed my words and turned his back to me so that I could wipe down his shirt. When I touched the cold, wet cloth to his back the first time, he shivered and I winced. "Sorry," I said.

"It's fine. Just cold."

When I was convinced that I had gotten everything off of his shirt, he turned around and stepped closer to me. I swallowed noisily, nervous.

"You missed something," he said, almost a whisper. He touched his thumb to my cheek, wiping off the last of the glowing fireflies. He left his hand on my cheek and, without warning, touched his lips to mine. Softly, softly.

He pulled back and looked into my eyes for moment, then leaned down to me for another. My heart was fluttering in my chest, and my hands were shaking at my sides. His scruff had grown in a little, much like Kale's, so it scratched against my cheek. He parted my lips with his own, and pulled his hands up to tangle them into my hair. My own arms looped around his neck, and we kissed for a moment. Until I remembered what we were doing. Where we were. Who I was.

I pulled back and looked away from him, not wanting to see that hurt look that was bound to be in his eyes. I closed my own eyes and bit my lower lip, trying to calm myself down and forget everything that had just happened. We couldn't do this. Not then. Not ever, anymore.

Turning my back to him, I walked away at a brisk pace, my eyes trained on the floor. I glanced up to see Kale and Lynne looking back and forth between me and Nate. Kale had a look of anger in his eyes, and from Lynne, there was a look of awe. I snatched up my bag and ran up the flight of wooden stairs opposite from the front of the barn. I shoved my pack to the floor and took in my surroundings.

I thought this must be where they had stored the hay, because the whole top floor was covered in the stuff, and it smelled like wet straw. I touched the hay, making sure it wasn't wet, and opened my pack to get out my blanket and extra clothes from my pillowcase. I could hear Kale, Nate and Lynne below, speaking in hushed voices. Probably deciding who would be best to send up and make sure I was okay to be around before they could settle in too.

I hurried up and lay down on the hay and I had just pulled the blanket over me when I heard footsteps coming up the wooden staircase. They sounded heavier, so they were definitely not Lynne's, and I found it highly unlikely that they would send Kale up, so it must have been Nate's footfalls that were carrying through the barn. Once he got to the top of the stairs, I heard him call out, "Alex?"

I didn't say anything. He knew I wasn't asleep, so he knew I must have been ignoring him. He walked over to beside where I was lying and knelt beside me. "Alex? I know that you are awake." Still not speaking, I gave him a sigh to tell him that I realized that, and that I didn't care. I expected him to try to shake me, or to try and turn me over so that I'd look at him, or just to go away.

As it turned out, he did none of the three. He did something that I really never expected him to do.

He *apologized*.

"Alex, I'm sorry, about the kiss, and just everything. I didn't mean for it to get carried away. I thought that I had felt something between the two of us but I know that you and Kale found us after you found each other, and I didn't realize that something might have been going on between you two and I am sorry. Really. I know I might have messed something up. So I'm sorry if I did."

He got up, and I heard him walking away. *I* felt really guilty that *he* felt really guilty. I turned over and said, "Wait, Nate. Come back over here." He paused, his foot hovering over the top stair, and turned around.

I pushed myself up into sitting position as he walked back over to me. In the faint moonlight, I saw the pink staining his cheeks, and the yellow firefly juices still glowing on his black shirt. His face showed concern, and this made me feel even guiltier.

"Are you okay?" he asked me, and I winced. Just the fact that he cared was enough to make me feel worse about myself.

"I'm fine," I answered, pulling the blanket up over my legs.

"Then why did you run away like you were disgusted, or even, forgive me for saying this, scared?"

I looked down again, picking at the fuzzes on the blanket. "I wasn't disgusted," I mumbled, and I saw his look of surprise out of the corner of my eye.

"You were scared?" he asked.

I nodded.

"What were you scared of, Alex? You know that I wouldn't..." he started.

But I interrupted him with: "It wasn't anything you did, or anything you could've done." I looked up. "What happened to your parents?" I asked.

The question took him by surprise. "My parents are dead. Or, more like they are *undead*. They were bitten by a zombie in the first month of the sickness. I didn't have the heart to kill them then. I wish I had now. Why?"

"Did it hurt when they were…um…gone? Did you cry? Did it hurt to lose them?" I asked, masking my voice the best I could to keep him from knowing that I was about to cry.

"Well, yeah," he answered. "Didn't it hurt when you lost your parents?"

I cringed. "I didn't know my parents. They didn't care about me either. I have no idea who they were. My grandmamma raised me. She doesn't…she didn't like to talk about my mother, her daughter, or my father, so I'm assuming they were both dead when the whole apocalypse thing came into play."

"Well what about your grandmother?" he asked. I looked away again. I'd known this question would come up. I'd known it would – sometime or another.

"Grandmamma was bitten," I said, a quiver in my voice, the whole story coming to mind once again – the story that I just couldn't seem to leave behind. "She was outside in her garden – we lived in a gated community, she thought we were safe – when my neighbor's daughter, Janie, comes outside. Grandmamma couldn't see well, so she didn't know Janie was infected. Janie bit Grandmamma, and I heard her scream. I ran outside, and hit Janie with a shovel. I stayed with Grandmamma, took her inside, and wrapped her in blankets. I locked her in her room that night. When I woke the next morning, she was in her room looking out the window at the neighbor's house. When she heard me come in, she lunged. But I was prepared. I had Papa's gun." A tear leaked from my eye.

"After she was dead, I stole my Papa's guns, packed some food, and took off. For a week or so, I was a mess. I was starved because I was afraid to stop and scavenge for food. I didn't have any protection. I didn't even know how to use the guns I stole. Eventually, I learned to eat small meals, and to avoid the flesh-eaters all together. I learned to use the guns, learned how to make no sound, learned how to look for food in houses and use that food while on the run. I haven't stopped moving since."

Finally. I'd finally gotten the story out. Somebody finally got the story out of me. "Oh, Alex, I'm sorry. I didn't mean..." He didn't finish his sentence. He tried to wipe the tear off of my cheek, and I shied away. He might have gotten the story out of me, but he was not going to get close to me. Especially not now.

"Good night, Nate," I said in barely a whisper, and he stood up. "Can you tell them that I'm sleeping?" I asked him. I didn't want them to know that I was crying.

"Sure," he said, walking away. His foot hovered over the top of the step before I called out his name again. He turned around.

I gave a smirk. "There is nothing, I repeat, *nothing* between Kale and I," I said, and I watched him walk down the stairs, a small smile on his face.

****

When I woke up in the morning, everybody else was awake and packed up, ready to leave. I smelled smoke coming from the main room of the barn. I stretched out my limbs, using this small moment of time to collect my thoughts and get myself together.

I got my extra shirt out of my pillowcase and changed into it, leaving my tank top on underneath. I searched my bag for my extra pair of jeans but remembered I'd given them to Lynne when her pants became too ripped to wear. I just stayed in the jeans that I was wearing.

I stuffed my pillowcase and blanket back into my pack, and I was checking the amount of ammo I had when I heard somebody at the top of the stairs. I whipped around and saw that it was just Nate. He'd obviously just woken up himself, because his hair was standing up straight in the back, and I thought I could see just a little bit of drool on the side of his chin. I smiled at him awkwardly.

He smiled back and walked over to me. "I just came up here to wake you up. We are all leaving."

"Thanks," I said, "but my internal alarm clock and the smoke beat you to it." I shoved everything else back into the bag, shouldered it, and turned back around to him. "Okay, I'm ready." I tried to walk past him down the stairs, but he stopped me. I sighed and looked down at the floor. He was not going to make this easy, was he? He put his hand underneath my chin and forced me to look up at him. There was a sour look on my face.

"Are you okay?" he asked.

Again, that question. Just like last night. "Yes, Nate," I answered. "I'm just fine."

The look he gave me told me that he didn't believe me. What did he care? Why did he care?

"Alex, you just broke down crying last night. You have gotta be the toughest girl I know, and tough girls don't break down crying because of nothing. Look, I'm sorry if I came on too strong last night but…"

I stopped him with a look. "Nate…it was nothing that you did. Well, actually, it's related but it wasn't the fact that you kissed me. Or that you came on too strong, which I can say, you did not. I kissed you back with just as much emotion as you kissed me. It's just…" I stopped. I didn't want to explain this. Not now. Not ever. Especially not to a boy. Man. Whatever.

Apparently, he mistook my hesitancy as something that it wasn't because he turned away and said, "It's fine, Alex. If that is how you feel then I'll just stay away from you."

He started walking down the stairs but I grabbed his arm and made him face me. "Nathan. Sorry, Nate. It isn't that I don't like you…that way, it's just…I don't want to get close to anybody."

His face softened out of the grimace that he usually only got when fighting flesh-eaters.

"In this world…" I started, "getting close to someone is the last thing that I would want to do. Because something, or someone, could just take it all away in a matter of seconds. Even though I never met you or your sister until three days ago and you never tried to get close to me in that time, I still felt like there was something that you…didn't hold back, in that kiss. Like you put all of your emotions and feelings into that kiss. And when I looked into your eyes after, I could see the lust, the want in them. As much as I want to deny it," I looked down, "I felt that too, and it is too much for this new world. Too much to be taken away too easily."

I didn't have to look up to know that his face was like stunned silence. That he was processing all the information I'd just given him. So before he could say anything, I pushed past him and walked down the stairs, wiping my face clean of emotion and putting on the indifferent mask that I had on every other day.

CHAPTER 14

By the time Nate got all of his emotions together and went downstairs, Lynne, Kale and I were packed and ready to head to the next location. So Nate grabbed his stuff from where he'd dropped it at the top of the steps.

"It's 'bout time you guys got down here," Kale said. I could tell he was still resentful for the way Nate had kissed me last night. I avoided his gaze by pushing open the big barn door and taking a step outside.

"Alex?" I heard Lynne call out, and I turned around. "What are you doing?"

I had to make up an excuse, so I came up with, "Scouting the area. Can't have flesh-eaters on our trail, right?"

She pondered this for a moment and seemed to decide it was a good enough excuse.

"Okay. Be careful," she said, and turned to Kale. She started playing with her hair and talking to him, and I rolled my eyes. Could she be any more obvious?

I walked outside to a chilly day. Looked like fall was finally coming. There was a breeze that blew the plants that surrounded us into a painting of great colors; something an artist would brush onto rough canvas with a palette in hand and an idea trapped in his head. Oranges, reds, yellows, purples, and greens, all brushed into one great masterpiece that ultimately smelled like fresh soil, and yes, more hay.

I walked behind the barn to investigate the woods line that started fifty feet away, when I heard a snap coming from behind me. Whipping around, I pulled out my gun, ready to shoot.

There was nothing there. I scanned the area, listening for anything off and looking around for something that might harm me. I saw a flash of white right beside my foot, and I shot it, killing the rodent.

I picked it up. A rabbit. Great, I wasted a good bullet on a rabbit, when I could have just stuck a knife in it. Yeah, it was good food but it was a small one, so it would probably only feed two of us. I rushed back inside the barn to see Lynne in full panic mode. "Alex!" she yelled as she ran over to me and gave me a big hug, avoiding the bloody rabbit in my hand. "Thank God you're okay! I heard the gunshot and thought maybe a daywalker got you!"

I sloughed her off and said, "I'm fine," before throwing the rabbit at the floor at Kale's feet. "Look what you have to skin and dry before we leave," I said, and he shot me a reproachful look.

"Why me?" he asked, kicking the little bunny.

"Hey, be careful with that," I scolded. "And you have to do it because nobody else knows how to make rabbit jerky."

He looked at me like I was crazy. "Rabbit jerky?"

"Yes, rabbit jerky. There isn't enough there for everyone to have a good-enough portion, so we can make jerky so that we all have at least one piece of jerky to munch on next week." I gave him a look that said, 'Do it or leave it out for flesh-eaters to get on our trail.'

He said, "Fine."

Now, I could bash some zombies' faces in but I could not watch when Kale skinned his animals and chopped them up. Nope, couldn't do it. And neither could Lynne, apparently, so we both went outside and were just talking about where we thought we would be if the plague hadn't taken over everybody's lives.

"Me?" I laughed. "I would probably be in school…it is around nine, right? So I would be in English class with Mrs. Lebornasky. I hated her. She would always assign us the longest assignments. Like, 150 pages to read in only one night. It was terrible."

"Well," started Lynne," I would probably be in school too. But, right now? We would be at mass." I stared at her. "What?" she asked.

"I'm just baffled. I could not imagine you and Nate going to a Catholic school. Did you have to wear uniforms? Like, Hogwarts?" I laughed.

"First off, Nate didn't go to the same school as me. It was an all-girls Catholic school."

You see, I wasn't a really religious person. Grandmamma had thought that religion was something to shove down somebody's throat, but that isn't what I thought. I thought religion was something to blame when something bad happened. Or something to praise when something really good happened.

"And yes, I did have to wear Hogwarts-like uniforms," she said, crashing my train of thought. I looked over to her and saw her holding a small yellow flower. I remembered my grandmamma telling me it was called a buttercup. Lynn smelled the flower and I could imagine her sitting with friends behind the school, carefree and happy. Now she was weighed down by grief and just…things that no person should have had to go through. I should know.

I nudged her and said," Hey," and she looked up at me. "Did you have a boyfriend that you saw in the summer back home?" I asked her, a friendly tone in my voice. She blushed and ducked her head. "No, but…I did one summer."

"Ooooohhhhhhhhh!" I said. "Was he your first kiss?"

She blushed harder and nodded and I gave out a sound that was a bit like a giggle, but it was also like an 'I'm-telling-Mom' kind of tone.

She pushed me, and said, "What about you? Did you ever have a boyfriend?"

I shook my head, still laughing. "Nope! I've never kissed a boy either."

She gave me a strange look, and then I realized what I'd just said. I *had* kissed a boy, but that was after the whole apocalypse thing happened. "Well, not before…you know, everybody was dying left and right."

She nodded and looked at me. "Alex, my brother…" she started and thank God, before she could say more, Kale was calling us to the front of the barn to leave.

"Great talk," I said to her and took up a light jog to catch up with the boys. I had never really talked to Lynne, just the two of us. She might have been a bit girly and a bit squeamish, but I thought that she could really make it in this world. Not the way Kale, Nate or I could. Not by shooting people or beating them up with a crowbar, but in a way that most people never really think of.

By being a good person. A good friend.

CHAPTER 15

When we walked, we didn't really talk. We just thought to ourselves and watched the countryside go by. I liked imagining what the place would have looked like before the apocalypse. In the cities, I saw people, endless amounts of people, and in the suburbs, I imagined perfect little lawns and mailboxes painted black. I liked it best, however, when we walked through the countryside, because it was nothing like the rest of the world, which was twisted and burnt by the hands of the illness. It was always perfectly preserved and I had no problem imagining how it used to be. Quiet. Serene. Just like it was now. That is, until we encountered flesh-eaters.

We walked for around five hours, stopped for lunch, then kept going. After around a total of eleven hours of walking, stopping to catch our breath, and pee, and killing only four flesh-eaters, the sun began to go down and it started to get colder. We all dropped into the grass, exhausted.

"Who wants to get the wood for the fire?" asked Kale. Nobody really wanted to, but we had to, so Lynne and I volunteered. We got the wood from a tree that had fallen just a hundred yards away. We sawed off branches with our hunting knives and carried it back to where we'd left Nate and Kale. They seemed to be in quite a serious conversation because they were both using their hands to gesture and we could hear them from thirty yards away. They were obviously arguing about something but we couldn't hear exactly what from where we were.

Lynne didn't seem to care but I was curious, so I tuned my hearing in their direction and hoped for a familiar word. I didn't hear one even remotely familiar word by the time Nate saw me and told Kale we were almost back to "camp." Lynne and I collapsed on the ground, exhausted.

I took the pack off my back and grabbed my canteen. It was almost empty. We would all have to fill up tomorrow at a stream or something. I drank it dry, then grabbed a piece of dried fruit out of a little bag that came from the inn that I was staying in before I met Kale. I gave everyone a piece because nobody had much food. Not anymore. We'd been walking out of sight of any houses for too long.

I didn't quite know what kind of fruit it was. Maybe mango? I didn't know. I practically inhaled it, so I didn't have time to figure out what it was. It was sweet, and sugary tasting. It reminded me of the tea that Grandmamma used to make me before bed. What was it? Apricot tea? Yes, that must be what I'd just eaten, a dried apricot. I closed my eyes and smiled, remembering how Grandmamma used to scold me for not drinking all of my tea. I laughed and summoned up a picture of her in my mind's eye but her chubby, pointing finger turned wrinkled and dry, and when I looked back up to her face, it was sagging and wrinkly as well. Her mouth opened, showing gray teeth that fell out of her mouth to reveal sharp fangs that grew in place of them, and she lunged forward, trying to grab me. I felt her teeth close around my shoulder…

I bolted upright, smacking my face off of somebody's forehead. "Ow," I said, grabbing my nose, which started to gush blood.

"Ow yourself," I heard Nate say, holding his forehead. I looked around for my bag and spotted it five feet away from the fire, at the end of Lynne's "bed," which was right next to where Kale was lying, with his pack under his head.

I tip-toed over to Lynne's bed, grabbed my bag, and tip-toed back to where I'd been lying. I grabbed my pillowcase with one hand, trying not to get any blood on it, and wrenched out the red shirt to staunch the flow of blood. Nate was sitting beside me, and it hadn't been my Grandmamma's fangs that were digging into my shoulder, it was Nate's hand, trying to shake me awake.

Nate moved from beside where I was lying, back to where he must have been sitting guard by the fire. I made a quick decision and got up to go sit beside him. He didn't even look at me when I sat down, which meant he was probably lost in thought. Already, he was back to what he'd been doing before, without even a trace of distraction. I admired that.

When the blood coming out of my nose slowed to a small trickle, I removed the shirt from my face and threw it into the crackling fire. The embers that rose into the air startled Nate from his little thinking stupor, and he seemed startled to see me sitting beside him.

"Hey. I was just expecting you to go back to sleep," he said, poking the fire with a stick and still not looking at me.

"Well, after a nightmare where your Grandmamma tries to bite your shoulder, it isn't exactly easy to get sleepy again." I shivered.

"Here," Nate said, taking off his coat and throwing it around my shoulders.

I accepted it only because I knew he wouldn't let me not take it, and, well, I was cold.

"Thanks," I said, pulling it tighter around me. "Are you keeping guard?" It was an obvious question that I was using to start a conversation. He just looked at me and sighed. This was going to be another awkward conversation. "What was your life like before all this, Nate?" I asked.

He looked at me meaningfully before starting. "Well," he said, "I went to Greenwall Community High School, got As and Bs, was on the football team and the archery squad, and I still wasn't well liked. I was too…different." He looked up at me, then back to the ground, and I could tell he was done speaking.

I put a hand on his arm, one that he didn't shake off. "I know how that feels," I said, moving my hand back to my lap. "I moved six times in my life. Always a different school. Nobody liked me. Especially at my last school." I sighed. How come Nate could get all of this out of me so easily? How come I felt like I could trust him with my life? Those feeling were dangerous. As much as I enjoyed having someone that I trusted, it was dangerous. In fact, I wasn't so sure I even liked it that much.

"Why didn't they like *you?*" Nate asked me, like I was the most likeable person alive.

I winced. "I, uh, kind of punched the most popular girl in school in the face."

He looked at me, then started to burst out laughing. I shushed him and pointed to Kale and Lynne, sleeping.

He quieted down to a small chuckle. "I'm sorry, I know it must have been rough for you, but that's why nobody liked you? You punched someone?"

I glared at him. Who was he to judge? "Well, if you punched Marissa Denary in the face then you wouldn't have been well liked either. And it isn't like I did it for no reason. Plus, you aren't the one with the blonde hair and green eyes." I shifted uncomfortably where I was sitting.

"Man," Nate said. "I must have grown up in a rough school because people got punched the face on a daily basis in my school. I was liked well enough that I wasn't the person getting punched but nobody really hung out with me."

"Why?" I asked.

"I was the poor kid. Nobody wanted to hang out with the poor kid."

I frowned, thinking. "But didn't your sister go to a private school? How did your parents get money for a private school? If you were poor, I mean."

"My mother and father are divorced," he began. "I lived with my mother, Lynne lived with my father. My father is an architect. He has lots of money. My mother is a teacher, who lives in a house in Brooklyn. Did live in a house in Brooklyn." He looked into the fire.

I knew how he felt. We lived in a small house and got clothes from the Salvation Army until Papa hit the lottery, and we could afford a nice house and nice clothes. "What happened when you found your mother as a flesh-eater?" I asked in a blunt voice, and he sighed, turning his head away from me. I put my hand back on his shoulder. "I'm sorry," I said. "I was just wondering. You don't have to tell me if you don't want to. I thought maybe..." I trailed off. "You know, I think it helps if you tell somebody. It helped me when I told you about Grandmamma."

I was just prying. It hadn't helped at all.

He turned his head back in my direction and glared at me. He knew I was lying. "Yeah, it really helps," he said harshly. "That's why you woke up with a nightmare where your grandmother tried to eat you." His tone caught me by surprise, and so did his mean words. I thought I felt hot rage working its way into my brain, but that wasn't it. It was sorrow. He'd broken me down. No, he hadn't. His words had. The truth was working its way into my mind, finding a place there, and taking root, creating direct lines to my tear ducts, and making tears flow out of my eyes.

I wasn't sobbing or anything yet, so we both sat in silence for about three minutes until he finally looked over and noticed that I was crying. "Oh, Alex," he said, putting an arm around me. This triggered the sobbing and gasping for air. "Alex, I'm so sorry, it's just...hard. You obviously know how I feel."

I leaned into him and put my head on his shoulder, putting my arms around his neck, and letting myself break down. I didn't care anymore. He seemed to care about me, so I guessed

I would let him. It would be his fault if he was broken up when I died.

I must have caught him by surprise because he didn't put his arms around me immediately. When he did, he didn't try to calm me down. He just shushed me a bit and hugged me closer, putting his head atop of mine.

He held me like that for I don't know how long. He held me like that until the sobbing subsided and the hiccups started intruding. He was sitting cross-legged, or Indian style, we used to call it, so I sat in his lap and rested my head on his chest, my legs hanging over the side of one leg. He ran his hands through my hair, trying to soothe me as best he could. When I found the courage, I said, "Thank you, Nate. That-hic-that has never happened. Oh, and I'm sorry about your shirt…" It had to be soaked through from all of my crying.

"It's okay Alex," he said. He was still running his hands through my hair, making me sleepy. I looked up into his face, and he was looking down at me.

I stretched my neck forward and gave him a peck on the lips. "Don't think that's because what I said yesterday was irrelevant," I said with a grin. "It's only for thanks." I started to get up, but he grabbed my hand and kept me from leaving. I turned and faced him, and he climbed to his feet as well.

He pulled me into a slow kiss, but I didn't kiss him back. I just stood there, without doing anything. When he pulled back, he smirked and said, "That's only for thanks. And, probably because I wanted to."

I turned away, not wanting to see the caring look on his face anymore. "Goodnight, Nate," I said and I walked over to my bag and made my bed. And this time when I dreamt, I didn't dream of my grandmamma. I dreamed of a better world, where Nate and I could be together, where we could sit in a meadow and just sit together, talking. Or kissing. Really, either would be just great.

CHAPTER 16

When I woke up in the morning, I was the first one to get up. Nate was passed-out by the fire, or what used to be the fire. Now it was just hot coals that were slightly smoking. I had to pee, so I walked to where Lynne and I got the wood and used the bathroom there. I walked back to the camp and Lynne was just waking up. I packed everything into my bag and sat there, waiting for everyone to wake up.

Once Lynne was fully awake and walking around, I offered her another piece of the dried apricot. She declined it. "My stomach isn't feeling well today."

As soon as she said that, I was on my feet. "Are you okay? Do you feel warm, or cold? Do you feel abnormally tired?" I was rushing around her, feeling her forehead, her cheeks – checking her pulse. "I feel fine, Alex," she said. "My stomach just hurts."

I wrinkled my nose. There were only three different reasons for her stomach hurting. 1) Gas, 2) She was sick, or 3) Cramps.

Oh, sweet Lord, I knew how those felt. "It's not...you know, cramps," she said. "I think it's just gas."

I narrowed my eyes and thought for a moment. "Okay," I said. "Sit down." I patted the ground next to me. She sat and started playing with a flower, like she had the morning before. I didn't recognize the flower. "What kind of flower is that?" I asked.

"Oh, it's just a wildflower. It's not even a flower; it's just weeds. They don't smell like anything though." She handed me the flower, and I picked at the petals.

"How do you know all this stuff about flowers?"

"On the weekends, before my parents divorced," started Lynne," my mother would take Nate and me out to the local gardens. I don't think Nate took in any of what she said but I thought it was interesting, so I remembered everything." I nodded. "Speaking of my brother," she said. "He is more fragile than he looks. I know that you may not realize it but he kind of likes you."

I rolled my eyes. Of course he did. "I understand, Lynne, and I know you care about your brother but I'm not going to hurt him. No, I'm not, because if we get too close in this hell, one of us is going to end up dying or *un*dying and that would hurt one of us. I can't get too close," I sighed, finishing my little rant.

We sat in silence for a few minutes until Kale woke up, and said, "Okay everybody. Today, we have to go on a food run."

Lynne and I looked at each other. Food run? There wasn't a town around for miles. I voiced my opinions and Kale shook his head.

"No, stupid. It isn't miles away, just about a mile." He smiled at me and stood up, stretching out his limbs.

"How do you know?" I asked him, a little curious. We usually didn't question Kale but when we did, there was always a better reason than curiosity.

Kale frowned and pointed to a little white dot in the distance that I assumed was a house. "That used to be my house," he said, letting his arm drop to his side. "I lived there, but I moved years before the sickness settled in." He grimaced.

There was probably a story behind the grimace, just like everybody had a story. The only one who had shared their story, however, was me.

"Okaaayyyy," I said, drawing it out. Then I walked over to where Nate was lying and motioned to the other two to be quiet. I crouched down and was planning to scare him awake when I felt something grab my ankle and make me lose my balance. I toppled backward with a sharp shriek and landed softly in the grass. I looked over to Lynne and Kale. They were trying not to laugh. Then I saw Nate's smile and I knew exactly what had happened.

"Nate!" I yelled with a laugh in my voice. I tried to roll him onto his back with my foot but as quick as lightning he grabbed it again, pulling me on top of him. I gave a little squeal and landed on his stomach, laughing on my way down. By now, we were all laughing and I sat on top of Nate's stomach like it was a stool. He laughed then rolled over, making me fall onto my back. Then he rolled on top of me and pinned me down. He started to go in for a kiss but I turned my face, all playfulness gone. He frowned, and then nodded, pulling me to my feet.

Lynne and Kale were still laughing pretty hard, so they must not have seen me reject Nate. I nudged him and start laughing again, making it as convincing as I could. He started laughing too and his laugh was so fake sounding that I actually laughed for real.

Once all of the giggling finally subsided and everybody's stomachs were hurting from laughter, we sat down and made sure we had everything packed up. Then, looking at Kale's old house, we turned right and started walking a ways. It must have been a hill that we were walking up, because after almost thirty minutes, my legs were starting to get tired. Once we reached the top of the hill, we saw Kale's old town.

"Town" wasn't really the word for it. More like city. Everybody except for Kale just stood at the crest of the hill, staring down at the massive buildings below. Everything looked broken down though, as if the heat wave from the summer had completely ruined the whole city. We walked towards it and I realized the city smelled worse than it looked. There were rotten garbage and dead bodies everywhere, creating a mixed stench of rotten eggs, decaying flesh, and sewage. We all pulled our shirts over our noses and forged ahead.

Right before we entered the city, we encountered a flesh-eater on the ground. It seemed to be already dead. Nate pulled out his machete and poked the body. Dead. He still stuck the knife through its head for good measure.

We all got out at least one gun or one knife; everybody but Lynne having out a combination of both. I stopped them before we walked any farther. "We have to make a plan, or something," I said. "This city could be overrun by flesh-eaters and there might be a gang somewhere in here." They all nodded in agreement.

"So what do we do?" asked Lynne, a bit skeptical.

I understood why. Unless we were looking for something specific, there wasn't much that we could do to form a plan. I looked at Kale. He shrugged.

"No plan then," I said. "Just watch your back."

"Lead the way, leader," Nate said to me. I laughed, then thought about what he had just said. Was I the leader? Was I responsible for the lives of my friends, no matter what? I guess I already was responsible for my friends' lives, just because I am their friend. Being the leader gives me no satisfaction.

We walked into the city, looking for a diner, a weapons shop, anything other than the giant office buildings that towered over us. I looked to the left and saw a sign that said "W p ns & rt lery" and headed down the street, the others following behind me. "They might have a crossbow in here," I said to them. I looked around the building and didn't see any people or flesh-eaters, so I opened the door and walked into the stuffy building.

We could tell that somebody already ransacked this place for everything they needed, because there were guns and bows on the floor and whole boxes of ammo had been tipped over and spilled. The knives that had been on the shelf in the very back of the room were gone, and nothing was left. We stepped carefully through the mess of bullets and broken glass, headed for the back counter. I checked behind it and underneath it, seeing nothing but a candy bar wrapper and rows of paper for the receipt machine.

I saw a door behind the counter and headed towards it, hoping that nobody had even touched the back room. Much to my dismay, the door was open a crack. I held my gun out in front of me and took a step inside of the door. I heard a

SWOOSH and felt something round, hard, and very heavy hit the back of my skull. I only had one little moment of pain before I passed out.

CHAPTER 17

I didn't know what had happened to the back of my head. All I knew was that now I had a headache. I considered trying to sit up, but the wisest thing was to stay down and pretend to be dead. That way nobody would attack me.

I heard gunshots that pierced my skull as if they were shooting at my head. I heard the sound of a blade on flesh, and people crying out in pain. I opened my eyes a crack to see Lynne fighting with a man who looked to be in his twenties or thirties. He was heavyset and bald, and he had a tattoo running down the side of his arm. I scanned the room some more to see Nate locked in combat with two men, both tall and skinny with sharp facial features. One had black hair and the other blonde. I wondered vaguely if they were brothers. I watched Nate weave his way in and out of their attacks. They weren't very good with knives.

I turned my head just the tiniest bit to see Kale in a shooting match with three men. He took them out with shots in the legs from his semi-automatic pistols and turned to help Nate. Before he could get across the room to help him, however, I saw the blonde man hit his mark with his knife and Nate cried out in pain. His right side was badly cut. He crumpled to the floor and I cringed. Kale shot the two men without them even turning around to see him. Lynne used the butt of her gun to hit her attacker in the face, and he crumpled as well. She closed her eyes before shooting him in the foot.

I understood. It was hard hurting people. But when they attacked you with what I assumed was a sledgehammer, well... something needed to be done. Lynne turned to see me on the floor and tried to help me to my feet. I stood up easily but my headache worsened into a migraine.

She and I ran to Nate, extremely worried. Kale was kneeling beside him, ripping Nate's shirt off so that he had easier access to the wound. I sat beside Nate and start to tear up. What if he didn't make it? What if he did but wouldn't be able to do everything he could before?

All these "What ifs" ran through my head as I knelt beside Lynne, who was just staring down at her brother. I turned to Kale. "What do we need?"

He checked the wound again. "We need antiseptic. Alcohol pads, Germ-X, anything that would qualify. Then we need bandages. I would prefer thick gauze, the white stuff, but it has to be really thick, or it won't work. I need a cotton pad, about the length of the wound, preferably longer. Then I would need a needle and the thickest thread that you could find for stitches. You got all of that?" He looked worried that I wasn't focused but I was. And I had one thing going through my mind. Save him.

I looked back at Kale and repeated the list back to him. I started to turn away but then turned back and got his attention once more. "Kale, do you think we could move him?" I asked. He looked at me, looked back at Nate, then back at me. "Probably," he answered. "Once we get him stitched up and bandaged." I nodded and then went to search for the supplies that might save Nate's life.

****

I ran through the city, combing it for a hospital or medical facility of some sort. Turning down a street, I saw an ambulance stopped in the middle of the road, the doors closed. I ran over to it, my head throbbing with each step, and tried to open the back doors. They didn't open on the first try, but I did manage to open them with the help of my knife.

Inside was a gurney that was missing a wheel, some rubber gloves, and gauze bandages. With some searching I also find alcohol pads, hidden away in a drawer beside the gurney. I left the gurney and shoved the supplies into my bag. Now I just needed the needle, the thread, and some cotton pad things. I ran in the opposite direction from where I found the ambulance, figuring if the ambulance came from the hospital and there was nobody inside, then it would be heading toward the problem and away from the hospital.

I ran down the road and took a left. The sky was darkening quickly. I didn't have time to search every block in the city! I saw a drugstore up ahead and figured I might find some needles there, maybe even some thread. Maybe I could get extra-strength Tylenol for Nate, too.

I forced open the door, searched the less-than-fully stocked shelves for anything that might help, and saw what looked like medical tape, so I grabbed it. I also saw T-shirts an aisle down. I sprinted to the T-Shirts and read the tags. 100% cotton. Perfect. I took around five shirts and stuffed them into my bag. Then I searched the aisles for needle and thread. Eventually, I did find some. The thread was even for stitching. I found Tylenol, some gum, some candy, and a bag to stuff everything in. I also picked up a small pack of water. We needed it desperately.

I ran back through the streets, trying to find the gun shop again, but also being careful not to be too loud. I found the weapons shop and pushed my way through to the back. Kale was still kneeling next to Nate, trying to make the bleeding stop, but it continued to gush out of Nate's side. I ripped the alcohol pads out of my bag and handed Kale the needle and thread first. Kale looked grave. He was having a hard time cleaning the wound with the blood gushing out of it.

I pulled the shirts out of my bag and used one to mop the blood off of Nate's side. Kale wiped it down more and laced the needle with the thread, his hands firm and steady. He then resumed his work, stitching the wound and pulling the flesh together. When he was finished and he tied off the thread, I handed him one of the cotton T-shirts and the gauze. He paused when he saw the shirt, but then he used it on the wound. I found the medical tape in the bag and handed it to Kale so that he could tape down the shirt without any trouble. He wrapped the gauze around Nate's torso, and taped that down too.

Kale sighed, looking at his handiwork, and then stood. "That is the best I can do," he said, and ran a bloody hand through his hair. I looked around for Lynne, and Kale's bag. Kale said, "I sent her away. She couldn't bear this. I told her to take all of our bags – except yours, you had yours – to close to where we spent the night last night. That way she wouldn't be all panicky because the worst she is going to see the wound is all bandaged up and white."

I stared at possibly the smartest man I have ever met and gave him a hug. "Thank you," I whispered, my voice shaking. When I pulled away, he nodded, and turned toward Nate, picking up his feet. He started to drag Nate towards the door, but he stopped when he heard Nate give out a groan. I rushed to Nate's side and shushed him. Kale sat next to me.

"We are never going to be able to move him without a stretcher or something," he said.

I looked over at him, then at the men who had attacked us. They were sitting, slouched against the wall, unconscious. "Would a gurney work?" I asked.

He nodded and thought for a moment. "Where is it?"

I tried to think. I hadn't really kept track of where I'd been going. I remembered taking two rights, but that was it. I told Kale and then started to stand up, assuming that I was the one who was going to go get the gurney.

Apparently my assumption was wrong. "No, Alex. I'll go. You stay here and...keep him company." His eyes flashed between my face and my hand, which was still resting on top of Nate's. I nodded, then looked back at Nate, whose face was scrunched up into a grimace. I felt the tears coming on. Fortunately, I held them back until Kale had left. Then I broke down, like every other time that I had been alone with Nick

"I'm so sorry," I said, sobbing. "I should have been more careful. I should have checked before going into that back room." I paused. "I shouldn't have let you think that I didn't care." I leaned forward and kissed his left cheek, the one that wasn't covered in blood.

I continued sobbing until the hiccups subsided. It had been an awfully long time since Kale left. I was about to get up and look for him when I heard the door open in the front room. I grabbed my gun off of the floor a few feet away and got close to the door but not so close that if it flew open it would hit me. Sure enough, it few open but it wasn't a thug that burst through the door with a gurney. It was just Kale.

Kale seemed hurried though. "Kale. What's wrong?" I ask.

He didn't look at me. "The people who tried to kill us? They were part of a much larger gang. The gang is coming to see if they are all right. We gotta get outta here." He tried to lift Nate by the arms, but needed help, so I hurried over and grabbed his legs, and together we lifted Nate onto the gurney. I used the straps and strapped him in so that he didn't fall, and I helped Kale push/carry the gurney out of the weapons shop. We hurried down the street that we came in on and when we got to the grass, we had to lift the gurney to keep it from snagging. I turned my head over my shoulder quickly to see if anybody was following us. I didn't see anyone.

When we got close to where we'd camped out the night before, we found Lynne lying on the ground, asleep. She had to be exhausted from the whole ordeal. I helped Kale lift Nate and set him on the ground, carefully. Kale collapsed beside Lynne and starts snoring. I wished that I could sleep, but I couldn't.

All I could do was stare at Nate and be happy that he was okay. Or, at the very least, that just then he was safe. I sat cross-legged beside him and brushed the hair from his forehead. It was long, and there were little streaks of black in it that I hadn't noticed before.

He groaned suddenly, with it decreasing in volume until it was but a small whimper. I frowned as I dug through my pack for the small bottle of Tylenol. I found it and unscrewed the lid, spilling out the contents into my hand. I took two of the small gel pills and slightly nudged Nate. His eyelids fluttered, but he did not wake up. I nudged him a little harder, being careful of his bandages, and whispered, "Nate? Nate, wake up."

Slowly, he opened his eyelids, revealing the deep-grey eyes that lay beneath them. His eyes focused on me, and he grimaced. Out of pain, or from seeing me too close to him, I do not know. I showed him the Tylenol. "I brought you these. I figured you would be in a lot of pain."

He nodded and tried to sit up, but failed and grimaced again. I pushed him down. "Rest," I said. "You'll need it." I handed him the pills and my canteen. He swallowed them, and then drained the canteen of water dry.

"Thanks," he said. He closed his eyes and sighed before saying, "That was not fun." He opened his eyes a crack and grinned at me.

I didn't return the smile. "This could have been avoided," I said. "If I had been more careful…"

"Stop," he cuts me off. He lifted his hand and put it on my foot. "Don't blame yourself. You blame yourself for everything."

I snorted before saying, "Yeah, but I'm 'the leader'. I'm supposed to keep you all safe. I definitely have not succeeded."

"Yeah, Alex, you are the leader. This means you need to be the strong one while everybody else is suffering. And in this new world, suffering is inevitable. So shut the hell up. You can't blame yourself for every little thing that goes wrong in the world."

I nodded my head. "You're right."

He smiled. "I'm happy you're okay," he said.

I stared at him, astounded. "Y-you," I stuttered, "What? You're happy that *I'm* okay, but you aren't even the slightest bit worried about yourself?" I shook my head. "You, my friend, are certainly selfless."

He frowned at the word friend and that made me worried. Did he think that we were something more? I tried to convince myself that this wasn't it but my heart was being contrary to my brain. "I am happy that you are okay," he said. "You could have had a concussion, or worse." He was right, again. I could have gotten a fairly bad injury but luckily the person who swung the sledgehammer didn't have much muscle. I still had a headache, nonetheless.

"Well, I'm happy that you are okay. You were hurt pretty badly back there."

"Yeah, it still hurts quite a bit," he said, shifting his abdomen and wincing.

"What can I do?" I asked and instantly regretted it when I saw his suspicious grin.

"I think you know what would make me feel better but I can tell you don't like that option." He sighed and I felt guilty. I did have feelings for him but even admitting it to myself was hard, and kissing him when he asked me would be like an instant one-way ticket to being a vulnerable mess.

He looked at me, and his face was almost a puppy-dog pouty face, but he was still smiling. My heart beat faster. My brain was saying, "Don't you dare do it, Alex," while my heart was saying, "Screw you, brain."

I decided to go with my heart.

I leaned in quickly, not thinking about it and not quite caring. Our lips touched and the effect was instantaneous. My breath quickened and, once more, I felt dizzy and weak. His taste of oranges and peppermint invaded my mouth. His lips moved silently with mine and he moved his left arm to the back of my head, twisting my hair into his hands. A million thoughts had been racing through my mind just a few minutes before, and now the only thing I could think about was his lips on mine, and his intoxicating taste.

I pulled back and shifted positions, so that I was sitting with my legs to the side and my hands on either side of his head. I leaned in again, being careful of his side, but he tried to sit up. I leaned back automatically when I saw him wince. "Nate," I warned, pulling my arms back to my side. He nodded his head.

"Do you want some more water?" I asked him, returning back to my casual demeanor. He sighed, then shook his head. "Well, do you want something to eat? I have some fruit strips in my pack." He shook his head again and I frowned. "Nate, you have to eat. You must be hungry."

He gave me a half-grin before saying, "I am hungry. Just not for food." My eyes widened and I was gaping. He chuckled at my reaction, and winced. I got up off of the ground, brushed off my jeans, and was about to walk over to my pack to make my bed when Nate grabbed my hand. "Wait, I'm sorry. Please don't go. You take my mind off of the pain."

I closed my eyes and turn around. I didn't want to hurt him further than I already had. "All right," I said, and sat back down next to him, but I just got right back up again. He looked sad, and I grinned. "I'm just getting my pack so that I have a pillow to lie on." I turned around and walked over to my pack but when I picked it up, it felt heavier than usual. I looked back to where Nate was lying. The very top of his head was facing me, and he couldn't see me at all. I opened my pack and got out everything inside.

I had one pack of dried fruit, an extra white shirt, my blanket and pillow case, one knife, my rifle and my other semi-automatic, the bag of "medical supplies," an empty water bottle that needed filling, and the candy and gum. There was also a folded up piece of paper that hadn't been there before. I grabbed the heavy, card-stock paper and unfolded it. Printed on it was a map of a city called "Resson." I studied the layout of the streets and the building numbers. Only the important buildings and street names were marked. I saw the hospital marked, and recognized the city immediately. It was the city not one mile from where we were camped out.

I studied the map some more. Here and there, house numbers were circled, some with red and some with green. I also saw two that were crossed out, and one with a star beside it. I was still studying the map when I heard Nate call out my name. Quickly, I packed up my guns, knife, the water bottle, and dried fruit back into my pack, grabbed my blanket and pillow case, and headed back over to Nate.

He saw the map in my hand his eyebrows pull together. "What's that?" he asks.

"I think it's a map of the city we were just in," I answered, and he held out his hand. I handed the map to him, and he looked at it while I lay my blanket down on the grass on his left side, next to the pillowcase. I lay down next to him and propped myself up on my elbow, studying his face while he concentrated on the map. His eyebrows were still furrowed as he held up the map straight in the air. His lips were pursed and his eyes were squinted in the dim light.

He looked back at me and frowned. "What do you think it is for?" he asked. I shrugged in reply. He went back to the map, and I smiled. I just adored how he could concentrate on his work so well. I reach my hand over and smoothed his furrowed eyebrows, but they just pulled back together again.

"I think..." he started. "I think it's a drug ring." My eyes widened. "Where did you get this?"

"I don't know," I said. "I was going to grab my pack and it was inside of it. How do you know it's a drug ring?"

He frowned and pointed at one of the circled addresses. "This is the weapon's shop where we just were. I remember the address. I also remember seeing white powder all over the place."

I thought about this possibility. A drug deal? Now? After the apocalypse? It seemed pointless to me, but I guess once you get into that kind of stuff you just can't stop. I looked at the map. "The circles must be where they deal the drugs...but what about the star?"

He cocked his head. "That must be where the supplier gives the dealers the drugs. Or, where they used to, anyway. They have to be dead, or undead by now." He looked at me. "What do you think?"

For about the fifth time, I shrugged before saying, "I dunno." I thought for a moment, then voiced my thoughts. "Why would they even bother? I mean, I know that they must be addicts, but seriously? Killing yourself with a useless substance while everybody around you is dying either from flesh-eaters or natural causes? It is sick."

He nodded and then chuckled. "I'm glad you will never kill me for drugs," he said, laughing. I yawned, and he chuckled again. "Come here." He lifted up his arm and pulled me close to his body. I snuggled into his good side and drank in his scent. Because we took showers four days ago, he didn't smell bad at all. Somehow, he seemed to keep smelling good even for that long a time. He smelled like he tasted, like peppermint and oranges, and I even detected a hint of chocolate. I smiled into his shirt and rested my head on his arm.

"I really am happy that you are okay," I said to him. He just sighed. I looked up into his face and saw that he was sleeping, his right arm still outstretched with the map in his hand. I stifled a laugh and I kissed his cheek before snuggling back into his side and falling asleep.

CHAPTER 18

The next morning I woke up with my butt backed up against Nate's side and his arm still underneath my head. I was about to close my eyes and fall back to sleep when I felt like there was somebody staring at me. I lifted my head and looked around to see Kale and Lynne staring at me with open mouths. Sitting up quickly, I was immediately nauseous. I sprang to my feet and ran ten feet before bending over and vomiting up what little contents were in my stomach.

I remembered this happening in the middle of the night as well. I was getting up to pee when the same thing happened. I also remembered washing my mouth out with Lynne's canteen.

I heard somebody walking up behind me while I was dry heaving into my shirt. "Alex?" I heard Kale say. "Are you all right?"

In between the spasms, I managed to choke out a "No" before the stomach acid started burning my throat again.

He walked over while I got on my hands and knees and spit up a bit of mucus and what I assumed was stomach acid. He saw me heave once more and said, "You need something in your stomach." I shook my head. Right then, I couldn't have eaten anything. "We all do," he said. "I'll go hunt for food. I'll send Lynne over while I pack up for the city. You three will stay here and watch over each other a bit."

I didn't have enough strength to shake my head in protest.

He walked away and the spasms slowed down. By the time Lynne walked over and sat down next to me, they were gone completely. "Are you okay?" she asked me. I nodded my head. She went to pat my back but I twisted away from her hand, keeping her from touching me. The last thing I needed was to cough and for it to start all over again. I got up and started walking back to camp, and Lynne had to jog to catch up to me. "Alex, wait!" she called out, and I stopped. She walked over, breathing a bit heavier than usual. "I need to talk to you."

I didn't need this now, I really didn't. Couldn't a girl be happy for two seconds and not care about anything else? *No, I think to myself. Stop thinking like that. You are Alex Grason, and you are in the apocalypse. Nothing can change that, and that means nothing will. You can complain when you are dead.*

I sighed and turned around. "What?" I asked, my voice a bit raspy. Shit. Raspy voice=unclear communication and planning, and unclear planning=injuries and death, as we witnessed back in the city.

Lynne seemed surprised when I turned around, like she wasn't expecting me to. "Hey, I know that we have all been through a lot, but you need to stop the act. Right now."

I looked at her funny. What in the world was she talking about?

"You keep messing around with my brother's head. Either decide on what you feel, or knock it the hell off because it is making me really pissed."

I stared at her, open mouthed. I had never heard her swear before. She stomped off before I could even reply to what she'd said. I walked back to camp in a daze. Is that what she thought? That I was trying to play hard to get with her brother? That I was trying to mess with his head to get a reaction out of him?

I didn't realize I was back at camp until I heard Nate call out, "Hey Alex. Come 'ere." I looked at him. He was in a sitting position, with my blanket still lying beside him. Kale had already left to look for food. I walked over to my blanket and sat down beside him, my head on the shoulder of his left arm. He wrapped this arm around me and pulled me closer, kissing my head. "Are you all right?" he asked.

I nodded and said, "I'm fine now," but my voice was still raspy, and I choked a little in the middle, making my eyes water.

He looks at me with a quirked eyebrow. "Really? Because you sound worse than I look," he laughed.

I smiled. Out of the corner of my eye, I saw Lynne sitting by her pack and glaring at me hatefully. Nate saw me gazing towards her and followed the line of my eyes. "Lynne, what are you doing?" he asked in a rather firm tone.

"I'm just looking at heartbreak waiting to happen," she retorted, tossing her hair over her shoulder and turning her back to us. Nate looked at me and shrugged in an I-don't-know sort of way. Then he winced, the shrug pulling at his stitches.

I frowned and clear my throat. "Quit that," I said in an almost-normal voice. "Too much movement will rip your stitches." I didn't know if that was actually true, but hey, safe is safe.

He gave me a half-smile. "Says you. Quit talking, you will lose your voice."

I nodded my head. This might be true as well, but if he was bluffing, he was doing a pretty good job of keeping quiet. With my head still on his shoulder, he ran his hand through my hair, and down my back. When he got closer to my waist, I stiffened, and he felt my body become rigid next to his. He looked into my eyes, and I tried to relax. I had never been this close to a guy, ever, especially not with my head on his shoulder.

"Hey, what's wrong?" Nate nudged me, his arm hugging me to his chest, my hair creating the perfect barrier between us.

"Nothing," I whispered back, and for good measure, I laced my hand with his. "I am just not very good at letting my guard down, even with the people I trust. Because of, you know…Grandmamma."

He gave a small chuckle. "You mean, letting yourself care about somebody who cares about you?" he asked.

I nodded my head for about the billionth time. Nate put his hand beneath my chin and pulled my chin up, forcing me to look at him. His eyes were hard, yet sympathetic. "You know that I don't care right? Hah, call me a risk-taker. What's that saying? 'It is better to have loved and to have lost than to have never loved at all?' Yeah, that's it. That's how I feel. Like even if I lose you, we got to be together anyway? To be able to say you were mine to cry over? That is a right that I would like to have, and one that I want you to have too." He released my chin, and I leaned back against his chest.

"I know," I said, turning my body so that my arms were around his waist and my face was in his shirt. He didn't reply, and just played with my hair while I thought about what would happen if I let my guard down and I did lose him. Would I cry? Probably. Would I be terribly heartbroken and be immobilized for a few days? Most likely, no. I liked to think of myself as strong, so hopefully that would never happen. Would it affect my view on the world as it was then? Maybe. The future was full of mysteries. I guessed I would open those doors when or if I came to them. My life was now about taking huge risks. This was one of my larger ones.

I decided to stop thinking about it. Because what was done was done, and what might happen nobody knew.

Nate and I sat with each other until Kale came back with two rabbits, a squirrel, and a handful of those dieting substances that make you feel full. Not the best haul but not the worst either. When he saw Nate and I, he respectfully looked away until I was up and making the fire to cook the food. Lynne, on the other hand, was probably staring at us the whole time, and processing all the worst outcomes that might crop up. Nate saw her staring once again and quirked an eyebrow in her direction. "Seriously, Lynne, what is your problem? Does it have to do with me?"

She glared at the two of us and then sighed. "No. It is your skank of a girlfriend who is the problem."

Nate's eyes widened at her vulgar language, then narrowed into slits. Kale whistled, surprised, then walked over to where I was still trying to get a fire going.

"Take that back," Nate growled but I blushed, avoiding looking at either of them. I might not have been looking at them but I could feel the tension in the air. Kale seemed to be acting as if he were deaf. He helped me get the fire going. There was a long pause before I finally turned around to see Nate and Lynne glaring at each other. Kale and I couldn't help but stare.

"I said to take. That. Back!" Nate yelled, pointing towards his sister. He couldn't get to his feet on his own but he tried anyway. His skin became as pale as a sheet. I rushed over to him and tried to calm him down. Lynne turned her back to us once again, a scowl on her face.

"Nate," I said, gently pushing him down to a comfortable sitting position. "Just let it go. I have been called worse before. It doesn't mat…"

"It does matter!" he interrupted. "She can't be happy for me…"

"I have no doubt in my mind that she is happy for you," I consoled him. "She just doesn't approve of who you are happy with. Besides, I'm technically not your girlfriend, am I?"

His brow furrowed. "No. I never asked you."

"Exactly," Kale interrupted with a smile. "I could still sweep her out from under your feet at any moment."

Nate grinned. "Yeah, right, that is totally gonna happen," he laughed and I relaxed. When Nate was distracted by Kale, I risked a glance towards Lynne's direction. Her face was full of disgust. Great, not only did I take her brother, but she also thought I stole her crush away from her. I might have. I'd never thought about it. I didn't find myself caring.

****

While Lynne was busying herself with finding some herbs to cook the rabbit with, Kale and I tended to Nate's wound. I grabbed the bag of extra supplies and sat next to Nate, like a nurse. Kale cleaned the wound with the water that he used to refill his canteen and one of the extra shirts that I got from the drugstore. "This looks good," he said, examining the stitches. "And your stitches seem to be intact. You haven't been in any pain at all?"

Nate shook his head.

I bit my nails when Kale frowned. "Can you feel this?" He gently pressed his hand to Nate's side, and Nate winced.

"Yes," he said through gritted teeth. "It hurts. Badly." He grabbed my hand and squeezed it tightly, cracking my knuckles. I gripped his hand as well. "How long will it take to be better?" he asked. "Until I can stand on my own?"

Kale had his brow furrowed. "Well, it was just yesterday when you were sliced in your side. The wound must have been shallow, because it seems to be healing quickly. You should be able to stand on your own soon. Even if it was a shallow wound, it should not have healed this quickly..." He frowned.

I hear a shuffle sound and twisted around quickly. "Um, Kale?" I said in a strained voice.

"Yes?"

"Do you think you could bandage that wound up quickly?"

"Hm, maybe," he said. "Why?" That's when he looked up and saw the twenty-or-so flesh-eaters walking in our direction.

Chapter 19

I ran to my pack, grabbed my semi-automatics, and checked the ammo. I should be good, but I would need to restock soon at another weapons shop. Sighing, I shoved one of the guns into the waistband of my jeans. I tucked the knives into the holsters on my belt.

Honestly, I was not surprised that the flesh-eaters had found us. We hadn't seen a flesh-eater in how many days? Four or five? It had been only a matter of time before they found us.

Looking back at Kale, I saw him trying to quickly re-bandage a panicking Nate. "Get him wrapped up and on the gurney!" I yelled at him. He nodded at me, and I glanced back at Lynne, who was getting her guns out, too. Then I quickly ran forward, and whipped out my knives. The first two flesh-eaters I ran in between – my arms outstretched with the knives in hand. I chopped their heads off and heard them hit the ground with a thud. That is when the fun began.

I put my knives away and pulled out both of my guns, looking behind me to see Lynne madly firing into the right side of the horde. She got about one flesh-eater for every six bullets. I sighed. Well, at least she was doing better.

Wanting to avoid her bullets that seem to be flying everywhere, I turned to the left and started running toward the fifteen flesh-eaters that were bumbling towards me. I shot with deadly accuracy – I almost always hit every flesh-eater in the eye. Most of them went down once they were shot, but some still stood, not feeling the bullet that had shredded their rotten flesh. I ran past the ones that remained upright and spun around quickly. One flesh-eater was only five feet away from me. I shot him and sent my knife into the one right behind him. Then I ran back through the horde, picking off the remaining handful.

Once my side was clear of flesh-eaters, I saw Lynne struggling to get them away from her. Some of them were close enough to touch her. Walking toward them slowly, I shot the one right in front of her. I also hit every one behind that one but two.

This made things easier for Lynne. She took a little longer to aim her gun but when able to look through her sight, that girl was dangerous with a shotgun. She shot the remaining two flesh-eaters and wiped her brow. I sighed. That was less fun than I'd imagined.

I'm going to admit something to you. I actually enjoyed the fight. Killing off the flesh-eaters that got in my way. Being able to protect my friends. Feeling the jerk of the gun in my hand, hearing the swish of the blade in the air – that satisfying thud that told you that the flesh-eater had hit the ground, actually dead this time. Like I said before, you have to enjoy the little things.

I looked over to Lynne and made eye contact. She gave me a deadly look. I just frowned. I didn't care what she said about me. The only thing that I cared about was that she made Nate angry and he could have hurt himself if Kale and I hadn't gotten him calmed down. We turned to see Kale with a grin on his face and our bags slung over his back. Nate was the gurney with a scowl on his face. He didn't like the gurney, I surmised.

I found the flesh-eater that I'd stuck a knife into and stepped on its chest, giving me the torque needed to pull the knife out of its skull. I pulled hard and felt a hand wrap around my ankle. Panicking, I tried to pull my foot away, my knives and weapons forgotten. I managed to kick it in the face, causing it to lose its hold on my foot. Quickly, I jumped to my feet and stomped the flesh-eater's head in, bashing the heel of my Carhart boots into its skull. It stopped trying to eat my foot and I assumed it was dead. I wiped my hand over my forehead, picked up my knife, and spit on the rancid creature for good measure.

CHAPTER 20

We walked back to the city in silence, the only sound coming from the rattling of the gurney and an occasional groan from Nate when he hit a pothole or bump. I walked beside him, my hand in his. Kale pushed the gurney, and Lynne walked in front of the three of us. She probably didn't feel like seeing me with Nate.

When we reached the first building on the outskirts of the city, we all stopped. "Well?" Lynne said with venom in her voice, her right arm crossed over her left. "What is the plan, Mrs. Commander? Or is everything going to go down like last time?"

Kale just stared, while Nate and I were glaring daggers.

I took a deep breath before saying in a cheery tone, "Well, I was thinking that you could go out ahead of us, like five or six feet, so that if a flesh-eater comes, you will be the first to know, because it will be gnawing your hand off."

She narrowed her eyes even further until it looked like they weren't even open. "Well, I don't have much meat on me so the first thing that would be eaten by a day-walker would be your fat a…"

"Girls!" Kale interrupted. "Hey now, get along." He looked at me. "If you can't lead properly, I promise you, I will take your place." He looked at Lynne next. "And you. What is your problem with her?" He touched my arm and I pulled away, glancing at Lynne. I didn't want to make matters worse.

"My problem with her," she started, "is that she throws herself at all of the boys, not regarding their feel…"

I went up in her face, with the fabric of her shirt gathered in my hand. "Feelings my, quote, 'fat ass.' You need to grow. Up!" I got my face closer to hers, speaking through my teeth now. "You are in the goddamn apocalypse. This isn't middle school. Yes, you are fourteen. I know this. But I am only one year older than you, and I have done a helluvalot more for this group than you have. You aren't at home. You aren't posting on Facebook about how so-and-so looked so fat today at school. You. Are. Here. Do NOT start drama, I am warning you. One more word out of your mouth about how slutty I am and how your brother deserves better and I am turning around and slapping that freckled face. Do you understand?"

My breath was ragged, and my knuckles were clenched so tight around her shirt that they were white. Lynne cowered away from me and shook all over. She nodded and I released her from my grip, shoving her a bit so that she fell down on her butt. I looked up at Kale, who was trying hard not to laugh. Nate, on the other hand, was frowning. He looked at me and nodded, as if he approved of what I'd done but not quite how I'd carried it out.

"So here is the plan," I said. Lynne got up but didn't look at anyone. "I will go out ahead, with Kale and Nate behind me, and Lynne at the back." I pulled the map out of the bag I'd retrieved from Kale, located what I was looking for, and turned the map around so that the rest of them could see it. "Here is the hotel," I pointed out, tapping my finger against the rough parchment. I looked at Kale.

"It's only about four blocks away from here," he said, scratching the back of his head.

I folded up the map, and put it away. "You tell me the moves to make, I make them."

****

We reached the hotel in ten minutes and we only encountered three flesh-eaters. I found this peculiar but it made a bit of sense. If drug dealers still inhabited the city, then I was not surprised that they would get rid of all of the flesh-eaters that they could. We saw some lying dead all over the streets, in cars, even hanging out of windows.

I made a shushing sound as I pushed the revolving door. It moved with a small creak. "I am going to find us some rooms and make sure that there aren't too many flesh-eaters. Don't come in until I come get you." They all gave a small nod of assent.

I pushed the revolving door around until I was inside of the lobby. When I saw a flesh-eater that standing right behind the glass counter, I thought of a corny joke. I was smiling when I shot the flesh-eater in the eye. "Checking in," I said, with a chuckle.

It would undoubtedly have been unwise to take the elevator, but I had to see if it actually worked. I pressed the button and the doors dinged open. That is when I decided that I would take the stairwell going up and the elevator going down.

There were only ten floors in this hotel. I decided to get my exercise and head up the stairwell to the top floor. At the very top, I pushed open the stairwell door and saw a fairly short hallway with only four doors – two on both sides and the elevator at the back. I tried the first door on the right side, room 1001, and it was locked. I tried the next door and it wasn't. Slowly, I opened the door and there was a flesh-eater immediately inside of the door. I shot it in the eye and dragged it away from the door. It was a woman, so she may have had clothes that would fit Lynne or me in a suitcase. I checked the rest of the living room. Empty. That's when I took in my surroundings.

The entire front and right walls were made of glass. There was a hot tub on my left and a large, flat screen MacroHolo sitting in front of a plush white sofa. There was a king-sized bed in the right corner, and a mini bar in the left corner. There was a door on the left wall, which I assumed was the bathroom. I saw the woman's luggage right beside the bed, and a bag of peanuts lying on the ground next to the minibar. Near the minibar was a small kitchen area, with a mini-fridge, a sink and an electric stove. She must have just checked into her room, because the bed was made. I backed out of the room, pulling the dead woman with me.

The next door I tried was open too, but it didn't have any flesh-eaters, just a maid cart and a messy bed. Other than that, the room was exactly the same as the first I'd tried. I smiled. Penthouse suites. Nice.

The last door I tried was locked. Looked like we were sharing rooms. I pressed the elevator button and held out my gun, ready for any flesh-eaters who might have been trapped in the elevator. The elevator dinged and the doors opened, revealing two flesh-eaters. I shot them both in the head, no problem. The elevator was creaky and the light flickered but other than that, it worked just fine. It was odd that the hotel had power. It must have had back-up generators.

The elevator dinged again on the bottom floor and I walked into the lobby. I was about to walk out the front door when, at the last minute, I decided to grab the master keys that are behind every front desk, so that we could lock our doors and if it was an emergency, we would all have access to each other's rooms. We could also unlock the two suites that were locked, so that our rooms didn't smell like death.

I walked out of the revolving doors and gestured for them to come inside. Kale looked at the gurney, then me, quirking an eyebrow. I gestured to a door that matched the front of a building, which had a handicap sticker on it. He nodded. "When you get inside," I said. "Follow me."

We entered the lobby and we all loaded into the elevator. I pressed the 10 button again. When the elevator dinged, I walked out, unlocked rooms 1001 and 1004, said, "We have to share the penthouse suites," and held up each master key, beaming.

"Why don't you and Nate share a room, Alex?" says Lynne, her voice small. I turn around, expecting to see her glaring at me again but she looks nonchalant.

"That is what was intended," I said, holding up the keys again. "These are for emergencies. If you just want to talk, knock. If there is something wrong, use this." I pressed the key into Lynne's hand without looking at her and smiled at each of them. "Pick your room, you two!"

They looked at each other, and Kale shrugged. Lynne pointed to 1004, the farthest room on the left. Kale followed her into the room. I pushed Nate's gurney into the opposite room and unstrapped him from it. He sat up slowly and I helped him stand. We carefully made our way over to the bed, where he sat down. A thin line of sweat had collected on his upper lip, and his face was pale.

"I'll be back," I whispered. I didn't know why I whispered. I exited the room through the open door then went into the room where the lady had been staying. I grabbed her rolling suitcase, pulled it into the room behind me, shut the door, and walked over to the bed, unzipping the suitcase. I laid it down on its back, then opened the top cover. Inside, the suitcase smelled like freshly-laundered clothing and deodorant. I pulled out the first thing my hand touched and deeply inhaled. You forget how laundry smells after a while, and this made me feel like I was at home.

Fortunately, it didn't look like the woman had any business meeting or anything, because there was only one dressy outfit inside the suitcase. The rest were size seven jeans, sweatpants, T-shirts, spaghetti-strap tank tops, a V-neck, bras, underwear, socks, and a flannel. She had flip-flops, size eight tennis shoes, ballerina flats, and heels. Not to mention her toiletry items. These included shampoo, conditioner, body soap, deodorant, a hair brush, a razor, a toothbrush, face wash, lotion, and hand-sanitizer. I looked over my jackpot with what I imagined was a hungry expression.

Nate, who was still slightly pale, smiled and said, "Awesome. Now we can wash our disgusting bodies again! Wow! Two showers in five or six days. I'm impressed." I smiled back at him and had started sorting through the clothes when Nate put a hand on my arm and said, "You should bring my sister over here. She'll want some fresh clothes, too." I got up to go get Lynne, a scowl on my face.

I knocked on their door four times, waited for about a minute, and then knocked again. Again, I got no answer, and this worried me. I pulled out my gun and the key, and was ready to unlock the door when it flew open and Kale was standing in the doorway, breathless. He had a scowl on his face as well. He seemed angry at either me or Lynne. "What do you *want?*" he snapped at me. "We didn't open the door for a reason."

Wow, something must have been happening. Something that made me a bit worried. "I just found a suitcase with clothes in it. I was wondering if Lynne wanted to come and choose some for herself, if she finds some that fit her well enough. But I can see..."

"No! I'll come!" said Lynne, suddenly appearing behind Kale's shoulder. I stifled a laugh. Of course. She was such a girly girl, that she still got excited when getting new clothes. I thought of shopping sprees in the mall with Grandmamma and sighed. I didn't dislike them but they weren't my favorite thing to do. Now I wished that I could do that as much as I did it then.

Lynne walked out in front of Kale and seemed flustered but I didn't think anything of it at the moment. I thought that maybe it was because I'd scolded her for her elementary-school behavior earlier. I led her into my room where Nate was still sitting on the bed, waiting for us to come back in. I sat down next to him on his good side and he wrapped an arm around my waist, pulling me closer to him. Lynne sat down cross-legged like a child, on the floor beside the suitcase and started sifting through the clothing.

She pulled out a light-colored pair of jeans, a regular T-shirt, some sweatpants, a bra, socks, and underpants. She glanced at the lotion and then at me. I nodded to her, giving her permission that she didn't need. She thanked me and went back into her room to change. I grabbed a tank top, a flannel, a dark pair of jeans, a bra, underwear, and the V neck. That's when I took another look through the bag and noticed that Lynne had taken the dress shirt, too. I rolled my eyes. Typical Lynne.

I was about to stand up but then I decided to take the toiletry bag, too. A shower was precious and I really missed taking daily showers. I looked over my shoulder at Nate, offered him a grin, and then said, "I'm going to take a shower. I'll be back." He smiled, leaned back on the pillows, and crossed his arms behind his head. I headed for the bathroom.

The bathroom was in pristine condition. Not a spot on the tiled floor, the walls, the countertop or the shower. There were towels on the counter and on the towel rack, with small bottles of lotion, shampoo, conditioner, and body wash. It smelled like lime floor polish, and the cold tiles stuck to my feet. I turned on the shower and tested my hand underneath it, to see if there was enough electricity to heat the water. At first, it was cold, but it heated up eventually, to a warm-but-not-hot temperature that I found comfortable.

I washed my hair twice and I could practically see the dirt coming off of my scalp. I washed my body and shaved my legs and underarms while the conditioner was settling in my hair. Then I rinsed off, grabbed and towel and dried myself. I put the jeans on first. They were a little big, but I could always find a room where the unlucky owners had a belt. Then I decided to put on the V-Neck, because we would be in the hotel and we wouldn't be outside anytime soon. It was supposed to be loose-fitting, but the owner had been smaller than me so it stuck to my frame closely. That was the way I liked it, because the more loose clothing you had, the more likely you were to be pulled down by zombies. I pulled on the thick socks and left my boots in the bathroom. I wouldn't be needing them.

I towel dried my hair and noticed how long it had gotten. Before the apocalypse, it was a little past shoulder-length. Now it was down to my hips. I brushed through it easily, not hitting any knots. There was a little hair-dryer on the wall and I was about to blow-dry my hair when I decided to fishtail braid it instead. Grandmamma had taught me how when I was ten. I separated my hair into four parts and started to braid it down my back, making a herringbone pattern. At the end, I realize that I didn't have an elastic hair tie to tie it off with. So I just used my finger and made a small loop-knot at the end of the braid. I looked at my handiwork in the mirror then exited the bathroom, turning the light off.

I walked into the room and Nate was in the same position as he'd been in when I went to take a shower but with his eyes closed and his brow furrowed. I tip-toed to the far side of the bed and sat down, trying not to wake him. He opened his eyes nonetheless and took in my makeover. He whispered, "You look beautiful."

I rolled my eyes and lay down next to him. He struggled but eventually got turned toward me like I was to him. "I didn't mean to wake you," I said.

He laughed. "I wasn't asleep." He moved the arm on his bad side and reached behind my head, pulling the plait over my shoulder so that he could examine it. He touched the braid gently, like a parent stroking a baby's head.

I laugh. "You don't have to be so gentle with it," I said. "I knotted it, see? So that it won't come undone."

He picked up the knot and untied it. Then he started to work my hair out of its braid. I turned to my other side so that he could do this more easily. Once every plait was gone, I flipped onto my other side again.

Nate then said, "I like it down better, because then I can kiss you without having to worry about messing up your art. And you look more like you."

I rolled my eyes again as he pulled me in for a kiss. It was gentle, and tender. He broke the kiss to sit up, a struggle that I had to help him get through. Then he kissed me again but this time, it was heated. He moved his hands to the back of my head, twisting his fingers in my still-damp hair. I put my forearms on his shoulders, and my hands wrapped around his neck. He deepened the kiss, and I became a bit faint and dizzy. His hands moved from my hair, down my neck and shoulders and down my arms. I shivered.

He pulled back once again and kissed the line of my jaw, working his way down my neck and to my collarbone, where he stopped and reversed directions. He kissed my jaw once again, then looked me in the eyes and grinned. I grinned back and he put his hands on my shoulders and kissed me again but with much more intensity and passion. I felt his hands down my body, past my ribcage and bellybutton, and my own hands started to shake. I was just about to pull away and get air when I felt his hands start to work their way to the underneath of the hem of my shirt. I retreated instantly, leaping backward off of the bed and twisting my ankle. My ankle gave out from pain and I collapsed to the floor, breathing heavily.

Nate looked down at me from the bed with an apologetic expression on his face. "Alex, I'm sorry, I…"

I cut him off with a wave of my hand. "I understand. No need to apologize. If anything, I should be the one apologizing. I was raised with these weird, old traditions. It isn't like you were ripping off my shirt or anything."

"Yes, but that is how you were raised. My parents raised me nearly the same way. I mean, for Christ's sake, you're not even my girlfriend!" He raised his voice slightly with each word. I flinched and he sighed, then looked away, a sour look on his face. I got up and sat on his side of the bed. I limped a little, because of my ankle, but it wasn't the worst pain I had ever experienced.

"Well, would you like me to be your girlfriend?" I asked, a sly smile on my face, covering up my nerves. I was still shaking from the previous encounter.

He whipped his head up to look at me. Then the playful grin started to form on his face. "Well, what do you want, Miss Grason?" he asked, a false teacher tone in his voice.

I laughed. "Well, I'm pretty sure I want what you want," I answered, my face getting closer to his.

"Oh, yeah?" he said, our faces just an inch apart. We were breathing the same air, his spearmint and oranges breath making my mouth water. "Well what do you think I want?"

"I think you want me to be your girlfriend," I said, my lips so close to his that they were almost touching.

"And is that what you want as well?" he asked, leaning in so that his lips just barely brushed my lips when he asked.

Then with my lips gently pressed against his, I said, "I think everyone knows that is what we both want." And he pulled me into a long, deep kiss.

"Well, maybe not Lynne," I said finally, and he chuckled.

"Yeah, probably not her."

We kissed for a while and fell asleep together on the bed, our faces just centimeters apart.

Chapter 21

The smell of rice and vegetables cooking on the stovetop woke me. I reached my arm over without opening my eyes and felt the warm, unmade bed from Nate's side of the bed. I rolled over and squeezed my eyes tight before opening them.

The sun is filtering in through the clean, bright windows and it lit up the room. Judging by the position of the sun, it is about 9:00 am, give or take. I looked over to the kitchen area to see Nate standing by the stove on his own.

I was immediately propelled out of bed and walked over to him quickly. "What, exactly, do you think you are doing?" I asked.

He turned around slowly, then enveloped me in a hug. I inhaled his scent deeply. He had taken a shower, or at the very least, a sponge bath before I woke up. He smiled. "Cooking you breakfast in bed. Now, go get in bed, it's finished."

I refused to move. "I am not moving from this spot and letting you walk on your own to risk you falling and hurting yourself again. Yesterday you couldn't even stand at all without getting queasy and pale."

"I have to move slowly, but I can still move. And I think my wound looks better. Wanna see?"

I nod. He lifts up the side of his shirt to show me the stitched up wound. He didn't even have any dressings on it. Not that it needed it. It was almost completely healed.

I stared at his side, open-mouthed. "We have to get Kale," I said, already walking toward the door.

He grabbed a hold of my wrist and wouldn't let go. "Not until you eat breakfast in bed," he said, a playful smile on his face. I frowned but I knew he wouldn't give up. I moved with him over to the bed, and climbed underneath the covers, sitting up. He put the bowl of rice on my lap.

"All of this?" I asked. He nodded and I motioned for him to sit next to me. He did, and we shared the rice, eating every last grain. We ate silently and as soon as we were both finished, I hurried to the sink, put the bowl in it, and rushed to the door. I yanked it open and knocked hurriedly on Lynne and Kale's door. They pulled it open almost immediately.

"What's wrong?" asked Kale. I took a few steps back when I saw Lynne and Kale. Kale was in just his boxers, and Lynne was only wearing her underwear and the T-shirt.

I shook my head quickly and said, "Whoa there. Get dressed first, you two. I don't really care what you do but I don't think Nate would like this situation." Lynne blushed, and Kale just stiffened. "Come over as soon as you can." I walked away from their door, but I didn't go back in our room. I just paced in the little hallway until their door opened again not five minutes later when they were fully dressed. I motioned with my hand to come inside of the room.

Nate was sitting on the edge of the bed, nervously fidgeting with the hem of his shirt. He looked up when he saw us come into the room, and he smiled but not the way he had smiled earlier, when he demanded that I eat breakfast. It was a nervous smile, a nervous smile that made me nervous, too.

I sat on the bed next to him. "Tell them what's up," I said, lacing my fingers with his, trying to tell him, *It's okay, I'm here, nothing can go wrong,* without actually saying it out loud.

He sighed, then explained. "This morning I woke up with a dull pain in my side but it didn't hurt like it did yesterday. I took the Tylenol that Alex gave me. She took a shower last night, so then I felt grungy and gross, so I took a shower this morning. It stung but it didn't really hurt and it wasn't bleeding. I couldn't move very fast. But that is when I realized that I was up walking around without help. I didn't think much of it until Alex woke up and started to worry. I got really nervous." He was still fidgeting.

"Can you show me your stitches?" Kale asked. Nate pulled up his shirt. Lynne was trembling behind Kale, who studied the wound like a doctor, then looked up at Nate again. "May I touch it?" he asked, and Nate nodded. Kale touched the stitches and Nate winced but didn't cry out. I tightened my grip on his hand.

Finally, after another five minutes of studying the wound, Kale spoke. "You have healed abnormally fast. Has this ever happened before?" Nate shook his head. "Then that narrows down my conclusions. If he had always healed abnormally fast then he would have a condition where he had twice as many white blood cells than normal. But he hasn't had this since birth, so I only have two conclusions. The wound was either much shallower than we had thought, or..." he trailed off. He sighed before saying, "Or this whole apocalypse thing mutated you to heal abnormally fast. Have you felt like anything else was different recently?"

"No," Nate said. His hand tightened around my own so much that the bones in my fingers were being crushed but I didn't care. I just wanted to make sure he was okay. I looked up at his face. He looked like he was angry and confused. I looked at Lynne and tears were streaming down her face.

"Then I see nothing else wrong with you," said Kale. "Just be careful. Don't do too much too soon." Nate nodded. Kale turned around to see Lynne with tears on her face and he looked panic-stricken. I saw his arms twitch in her direction but he rethought his decision with a glance at Nate and didn't move them. He turned around and walked out the door, and I heard his door slam across the hall. Nate didn't move at all.

Lynne ran up to Nate, threw her arms around his neck, and cried into his shirt. As I moved away from the bed, he looked at me with a what-do-I-do look on his face. I smiled and shrugged.

She let out a sob and he shushed her. "I'm not dying!" he said with a laugh. "In fact, it's just the opposite."

She laughed too, and wiped her face. "I'm sorry," she said, sniffling. "But it isn't every day when you hear that your brother is some super-hero mutant!" She wiped her eyes again. "I'm happy that you are okay."

"Thanks, Lynne," he said and enveloped her in a hug.

She ended the hug and had started to head out of the open door when I stopped her. "Er Lynne?" I called out.

She spun around. "Yes?"

"Would you like to take a shower?" I asked. "We have shampoo and conditioner and body wash and stuff if you want to…" I trailed off.

She smiled thankfully. "I would love to take a shower. Thank you." I got the supplies from the bathroom and gave them to her. She thanked me again, headed into her room, and I remembered that Lynne and Kale might be together. I blushed at the thought. That's when I felt hands close to my ribcage and my fighter instincts kicked in. I whipped around and was about to punch my attacker in the face when I saw that it was just Nate, standing there with an eyebrow raised. I sighed and punched him on the good shoulder.

"Don't do that!" I said with the barest trace of laughter in my voice. "I almost punched you in the face." He laughed and I shook my head with a smile.

He pulled me in closer. "Well, you wouldn't want to mess up this pretty face would you?" he asked, making a strange face. I laughed and Nate kissed me deeply and slowly. He put his hands on my waist and I wrapped my arms around him and rested my head on his shoulder when he broke the kiss. He kissed the top of my head.

In that moment, I wished I could have frozen time forever. In the nice hotel room with a beautiful view, a perfect boy holding me, with our stomachs full and our bodies clean, I wished I could have frozen time. Because that moment was perfect and it was the best thing that could have happened with the unknown bearing down upon us.

We were in the hotel room for about five or six days. We raided the other rooms for food and supplies, killed off a flesh-eater or two in every room, and eventually found fresh clothes for the boys. I found a leather belt, and a pair of black leather boots that came up to around my knees, and I could fit my skinny-jeans inside of them.

Every night, I would fall asleep next to Nate, usually after we had been making out for a while. We talked about our families, what we missed, and what we would have wanted to do if the world were the same as before. He never got any further than lifting my shirt up the tiniest of amounts, to put his hands on my waist.

I loved how he liked to spend every minute with me. How he loved to cuddle with me on the fluffy bed. I loved how my touch could send his entire body into a violent shiver, and that he did the same for me. I loved when he played with my hair, and when I could smell his fresh shampoo right after he got out of the shower.

All of this ended on a Wednesday morning when Nate came out of the shower to find me awake and curled up into a little ball on the bed. He rushed over to me and asked, "What's wrong, babe?" and a tear slipped from my eye. He wiped it away and asked me again. I shook my head. It was embarrassing enough that he had to find me broken down because of *cramps*.

I'd had cramps before. This was actually not the worst I'd had. They had gotten so bad that Grandmamma took me to the doctor's every six months to get some weird shot thingy that stopped me from having any menstrual cycle at all. That was over seven months ago.

"Please, Alex," Nate pleaded, "tell me what's wrong."

He looked so worried about me that I had to tell him. Between spasms, I managed to choke out the word "cramps" before I had to wince again. The embarrassed look on his face would have been comical, had I not been curled into a ball of pain.

"Er, what, um…" he trailed off for a moment. "Do you want me to get Lynne in here?" he asked and I nodded vigorously.

Nate got up from the side of the bed and briskly walked out the door and I heard him frantically knocking on Kale and Lynne's door. His muffled voice mixed with Lynne's, and I heard their footsteps as they walked into the room.

Lynne crawled up next to me on the bed and got down to my eye level. "Are you okay?" she asked. I didn't acknowledge the question. She whispered to me, "Do you want me to go get you some supplies?" I nodded. She nodded as well and told Nate that she and Kale would be going to get my "supplies."

"No," he said, "I want to go, too."

I looked up to see Lynne looking at me, looking at Nate and her, and she whispered just loud enough for me to make out "here for her." Then I saw Nate nod and tell Lynne to be safe. She nodded back to him and left to get Kale. Nate walked over to the bed and sat next to me in an awkward position. He jostled the bed, and I gave out a groan.

He winced and said, "Sorry," but didn't move from the bed. We sat there in awkward silence for about five minutes, until I gave another groan and he slipped his hand into mine. He saw a tear streak my face and wiped it away. He brushed my hair from my forehead and kissed it, then lay down next to me on the bed, still holding my hand. I curled up next to him in agony and let the tears stream down my face and into his shirt. He rubbed my back.

We remained in this position, the cramps both getting better and worsening for about twenty minutes until we heard a crash outside of the door and Nate jumped to his feet, fumbling for his knife on the bed stand. I remained in my little ball of agony. Then the door flew open and Kale was standing in the doorway, two grocery bags in his hands. I closed my eyes as another wave came to knock my breath away.

"What happened? Where's Lynne?" I heard Nate ask. I opened my eyes through hot tears and saw Kale shake his head.

"We ran into a problem," he said. "Some people from the gang where we killed those bad guys at the gun shop ran into us while we were leaving the drugstore parking lot. They said something about a map? Lynne looked frightened and they saw the fear in her eyes I guess." He cleared his throat and choked out, "They took her. I got out of the situation in time to come back here and tell you the news."

So that was how the map got into my bag. Nate looked back at me, and I nodded. He explained to Kale that had found the map in my bag and that Lynne must have put it there. Kale paled, and Nate looked confused. Kale threw the bags to the floor at the foot of the bed and said, "I'll be back," before running into his room.

Nate threw me a skeptical look and searched through the bags, coming up with a bottle of extra-strength Midol. He read the back label and then gives me two and a cup of water. I throw both of them back and downed the water. Then, painfully and slowly, I got up and grabbed both bags and a pair of underwear that we'd looted and went into the bathroom. When I came out, Nate was searching through his bag frantically. When I asked him what was wrong, he said, "The map. It isn't in my bag or yours. It's gone."

CHAPTER 22

When the cramps settled down, I got dressed and pulled back my hair. Kale came into the room and started to pack up everyone's stuff. We didn't have to come to a conclusion to go get Lynne, we all knew that we had to. I got both of my pistols and stuck one of them into the waistband of my jeans while I held the other. The same situation went for my knives.

I turned to Nate, and he had two of his four knives at his waist with both of his guns, and the other two knives in his hands. Kale had his knives tucked into their holsters at his waist, preferring the guns in his hands. We all slung our bags over our backs and headed out into the street. I was going to miss this place.

We headed out onto the street, looking to Kale to show us where to go. He nodded his head to the left and we forged ahead down the silent road. We stepped carefully and lightly, making as little noise as possible. At the drugstore, we looked around the parking lot before stepping through the automatic doors, sticking together, trying not to be heard. We checked behind every shelf and even the checkout counter before heading back into the pharmacy area. As the door opened and made a loud creaking sound, I cringed.

Behind the door was just as expected – rows and rows of those bags with medicines in them. Except, instead of medicine in the bags, there was a white powder that vaguely looked like cocaine. This must have be the suppliers' "warehouse." I shuddered, and heard footsteps coming from the left. I whipped my head around to see five large men – all with the same tattoos on their forearms – walk into the room.

Quickly, I calculated the odds. Kale could take two and have them down to their knees in seconds in a fist fight, Nate could lock in battle with two with his knives, and I could only take one of them, with neither knives or fist-fighting being one of my strong suits.

I looked to the boys, they nodded at me, and we dispersed, each choosing a person to take on. I chose a fatter, shorter man with a handlebar mustache and a knife. I put my gun in my holster, but kept my knife out.

If you had been watching the fight, it would have looked ridiculous – a fifteen-year-old girl that doesn't weigh more than 120 pounds against a thirty-year-old man that looked like he weighed 300 pounds. I locked into battle with him when he took the first swing with his knife, I ducked, and threw a punch into his gut. It got him off balance, but he remained standing. His face was surprised but he aimed a good punch nonetheless.

His fist caught me in the jaw and I saw stars. I remained standing, though.

He tried slashing with his knife once more but I got in close and elbowed him in the face. He smelled like ketchup and garlic. Not to mention BO. Ew.

He held his nose to see blood coming from the right nostril. I was in a good position to stab him with my knife but as I went in for it, I got a particularly bad wave of cramps. I dropped my knife and bent over, clutching my stomach, momentarily forgetting where I was. The man swept my legs out from under me and pinned me down. He cocked back his right arm and punched me square in the nose, sending pain across my face and stars into my eyes. I blacked out.

****

I woke up and had no idea where I was. It looked like the basement of an old house and smelled of must and mildew. The dim light came from one small light bulb in the corner of the room and there was a door to my left. I heard people talking over the noise of a furnace in the adjoining room but I couldn't make out what they were saying.

I was strapped to a large wooden chair, like one might find in a library. My hands were tied with rope to the arms of the chair, and my feet were duct taped to the legs. There was a piece of cloth in my mouth, gagging me and soaking up all of my spit. My mouth was incredibly dry.

Wiggling my arms hurt. The rope chafed against my dry skin. Forget about the duct tape. That would hurt even worse. I tried to push the gag forward in my mouth with my tongue but it was tied tightly to the back of my head.

I was still struggling with the rope around my wrists when I heard the door open. When I looked up, a tall, average-sized, black-haired man wearing a suit came in. For some odd reason, he looked strangely familiar. He seemed surprised to see me awake, but happy nonetheless, flashing me a smile to which I glowered back. He made a *tsk-tsk* sound and said, "Alexandra. That is no way to treat your host." I froze when he said my name. How did he know my real name?

He laughed when he saw my worried expression. "How do I know your real name? Why, don't you remember me, Alex?" I shook my head. I had no idea who this strange man was. "Well, that's an easy one," he said. "Haven't you seen me before all of this happened?"

I shook my head again.

"I used to be your neighbor. Remember little Janie?"

I froze in my chair. Now I remembered him. This man was Mr. Simmions, my grandmother's neighbor. He had never been home much, he was always traveling. He'd been a businessman, and he worked for some huge company. Now I realized that his "huge company" was a drug ring. I gaped, forgetting about my bonds.

He laughed at my open mouth. "You see," he said, "I was home that day. Janie had been infected for about a week before you killed her. I had her in the living room, you see, and she somehow opened the door. I had gone to get her 'leash' we liked to call it, and I was watching from the upstairs window. I watched as you swung the shovel." His menacing smile faltered.

"I watched as she crumpled to the ground, dead." He took the gag out of my mouth. "What do you have to say for yourself, killing a nine-year-old girl?"

I curled my lip. "She was already dead." He smacked me hard across the face with his palm. It stung, but I continued. "If you had really loved her, you would have just shot her instead of keeping her caged up like an animal to suffer the life of a flesh-eater."

He smacked me again, this time with the back of his hand. "She was sick!" he yelled.

"She was dead," I retorted, my voice flat. "She was dead and you know it."

His eyes flashed with anger. "She was not dead. Dead is what you and your friends will be if you don't give me back my map."

My eyes widened. My friends. Oh my god. Kale, and Nate, and Lynne, oh Lynne. She had no idea how much trouble she had gotten us into.

"So you aren't going to kill me for 'killing' Janie?" I asked, trying to keep the fear out of my eyes.

"No. But I will torture you and that Nate boy for it."

"Don't touch him!" I snarled. "Don't you even think about it. Only me. I killed her. I get the punishment."

"I won't torture him like that!" he laughs. "I will torture you for Janie and him for the map."

"Don't touch him!" I repeated.

"I don't have to," he said, which threw me off guard. What did he mean, he didn't have to touch him?

"We don't have the map. I don't even know what you are talking about," I lied… unsuccessfully.

He sighed. "Oh, your friend is going to pay for that lie, sweetheart." I curled my lip in disgust at his nickname for me.

He looked at me with a frown and snapped his fingers. Two men appeared out of the shadows. "I don't like the way she is tied up," he said to them. "Put some duct tape around her midsection and the chair.

The crony on the left came up with a roll of tape from thin air. The one on the right held me down while the other one taped me up.

"That's better," Mr. Simmions said as a wave of cramps hit me hard. I gritted my teeth – I'd forgotten about those.

"Bring him in," Mr. Simmions said to the goons. They nodded their heads and they went into the other room. Who were they bringing in? A person to punish me with brass knuckles? Or perhaps, a baseball bat? No, the person they brought in would torture me much worse than physical pain. They brought in a brown-haired, grey-eyed someone, with bruises all over his face, who was duct-taped to a chair, like me.

They brought in Nate.

CHAPTER 23

"No!" I screamed when I saw him. Nate was conscious, but he didn't recognize me in the dim light. When he heard my screech, he realized who it was, and he struggled against the duct tape. "You aren't allowed to touch him!" I screamed.

Mr. Simmions got close to my face. His breath smelled like toothpaste. "What did I say? I said I wasn't going to touch him, did I say that? Yes, I did."

I spit in his face.

"Alex!" Nate called out, and it felt like my heart was going to explode. Mr. Simmions wiped my saliva off and smacked me hard across the face once again. When I heard Nate scream "Don't hurt her!" I finally realized how Simmions would punish both Nate and me at the same time. He would physically beat me, while Nate would be tortured by me being hurt. I almost died.

"Nate!" I called out for the first time. He responded with my name.

"Now," Mr. Simmions said. "I will bring in my men. Okay?" I curled my lip up in disgust. "Come on in, boys!" he called out, and one by one, the men filtered inside of the small room. Though all of them were big, some had different weapons. One had a baseball bat, another had brass knuckles, and yet another had a knife. Some of them came in with just their bare fists.

"No!" Nate screamed. I shook my head. He had to be quiet, or I would be in even more trouble. I knew I never should have fallen for Nate. I knew that it would be a bad idea, that one of us would get hurt, or one of us would die, and life would be a terrible mess. I wished I had trusted my instincts. Yet, I was also glad that I hadn't. I loved knowing Nate felt the way I did, that he could love the weak person that I was, that I had been able to feel his caress and know that he belonged to me and nobody else. But that was how we both got into this mess.

"Now, everybody get in a line," Mr. Simmions said, and the line curved around the room. The first man I saw had a bare fist. "Start!" Simmions said, and the line started to move. I closed my eyes so that I wouldn't know what was happening – so that I could pretend that this was somebody else, and not me. I felt his fist collide with my jaw and my head jerked to the side. I heard Nate screaming, and Mr. Simmions laughing.

"It will stop when you tell me where the map is," he said.

A crunch as a baseball bat collided with my stomach and I was gasping for air.

"We don't know!" Nate shouted as brass knuckles pounded my right eye in. I groaned and Nate screamed again. Another plain fist, jerking my head to the side. I spit out some blood and saw stars. Nate was still screaming and I heard a hysterical sob. I kept my head up, as fists and brass knuckles peppered my face with bruises. A blade of a knife cut into my cheek and I screamed into my gritted teeth. A pistol whipped me across the face and I spit out what I believed to be a tooth. I felt a warm, sticky liquid run down my face and onto my shirt but I refused to say that it was blood. Then, somebody decided that they wanted to be different. My head whipped backwards as an aluminum baseball bat hit my jaw. Blood and teeth spurted from my mouth as I gave out a whimper, then a sob. I saw stars and I opened my eyes to see blood running down my face and clothes.

I couldn't hear anything, which was weird – just a faint ringing. Nate was sobbing and screaming and struggling against his bonds. The room was spinning wildly. Black clouds were at the edges of my vision. I vaguely saw another man walk up to me with brass knuckles and cock his arm back, and I felt the pain explode across my jaw before I lost consciousness.

****

I woke up just like before, strapped to the wooden chair. What was different was that I felt cold water against my face and skin, and it stung. The room had emptied of Simmions's men, other than the one who was hosing me down. I also registered Nate tied to his chair, sobbing in the corner. Mr. Simmions was beside Nate, watching a big man hose me down. When he saw that I was awake, he said, "Stop," to the man. He walked up to me and got very close to my face.

"I'm going to ask you one. Last. Time. Where is the godforsaken map?" His voice was unnaturally level, which meant he was struggling to maintain his cool.

"May I ask you why you want this map so bad? Why you deal the drugs? What you get in return for them?" My voice sounded rough, like I had been gargling nails.

Mr. Simmions laughs. "What do I get in return? Well, not only do people pay me with food, medical supplies and protection, but I also get power. Power is what I am really after. They all fear me, not to mention rely most on me. People get hooked on these drugs and they can't stop, not even after the world has gone to hell, and I can control them like puppets on a string. And after this apocalypse is over and everything is back to normal, then they will know that I am the one who protected them and supplied them, and that I am the one that could take it all away with one bullet to the head. That is why I need that map. It shows all of the locations of where people deal drugs. I take them out, all of them, until I am the only one left. Understand why you have to give it to me, *now?*"

I shook my head, sending the world spinning again. "I already told you," I said with a mouthful of blood. "We don't have it." I spit the remaining amount of blood in his face and he cringed, frantically wiping the blood off himself. I smirked. He should have learned from the first time.

"You really are a disgusting little girl," he said, still trying to wipe the saliva and blood from his face. He paced around the room once more then pulled out a gun, pointing it at me.

"NO! Please, kill me instead, *please!*" Nate sobbed, and I could see no pity for him in the eyes of this evil, sick, twisted, and tortured man who stood before me.

I just laughed when I stared down the gun's barrel. "Really? Really, you pull a gun?" I continued to laugh, much to both Mr. Simmions' and Nate's surprise. "Go ahead," I told him. "Shoot me. I don't care. It could only get better once I leave this place right? I mean, we are in hell." A smirk lifted the corners of my lips. "So go ahead and do it. Shoot me. I hate this place anyway. I hate the lies, the torture, the death, the heartbreak, the sadness, the loss, the anger, and the spite.

"I hate the way humans have turned on humans, brother on sister, flesh on blood. Though, I do suppose it was already like that before the whole apocalypse thing, wasn't it?" I shook my head in disgust. "In this imperfect world, there is no winning. No, there really isn't. You can just survive. Survive one more day than the person who stands next to you – the person who is destined to die in the end anyway. This isn't living. It's surviving. And I can't help but wonder when those who I love will die. I don't want to see that day.

"This world? It isn't even a world. It is carnage. It is chaos. It isn't something worth dying for." I risked a glance in Nate's direction. He'd been silenced by a man who had a gun to his head, but his silent sobs were racking his body. The tears streamed down his face. *Don't do this, Alex,* he seemed to say to me. *Please don't do this to me.*

I closed my eyes and tried to compose myself again. "Nate," I called to him, not opening my eyes. Not wanting to see the heartbreak that I had caused him. "I am so sorry."

I turned my head back in the direction of Mr. Simmions and opened my eyes. "Well, sir?" I asked him politely. "Are you going to do it, or are you just going to stand there like a complete and total ass while you turn me into a martyr?"

A grin tipped the corners of his mouth upwards and I closed my eyes and braced for the shot.

Two things happened at once. The first thing that happened was Kale burst through the door, a gun in his hand. He shot Mr. Simmions, and he dropped. The second thing that happened, however, was that Simmions pulled the trigger of the gun in his hand.

CHAPTER 24

It didn't hit me in the head, where he intended it to. Kale's bullet hit him just before he pulled the trigger, so he was on his way down when it happened. His bullet hit my shoulder, right above my heart, instead. I felt white hot pain spread throughout my body, originating in my shoulder. I gave out a groan. My breath quickened. The edges of my vision were blurry again, and I couldn't see straight. I heard another gunshot, and a large body hitting the concrete floor. Somebody was cutting the rope around my wrists and the duct tape around my ankles. When they got to my waist, I groaned and they shushed me.

The pain was unbearable. It felt like somebody was tearing at my skin from the inside, trying to get out. My heart pounded, trying to make up for the blood I was losing, but it just leaked out of my wound even faster. My breathing increased even more so that I was nearly hyperventilating.

They got me cut out and they moved me to the floor. I cried out in pain when I moved and when my shoulder hit the floor.

I blinked away tears, my eyes watering badly. Then I saw Nate kneeling beside me, tears running down his face as well. They splashed onto my skin, the warm salt burning the cuts on my face.

I saw his lips moving, but I could only hear a few words of what he was saying: "You're okay...please, *please* don't leave me...never say that...would die if you died...I love you..."

I gasped and started to pant. Fire was rushing through my limbs and I saw Kale inject a drug into me with a needle. Suddenly, everything looked abnormally bright, and sounds become booming and loud. I felt Nate's hand in mine and I cried out as the fire spread to my shoulder. His grip tightened. I tried to say something to him but was interrupted with a cough that turned to a gurgle as I spat up blood. He shushed me and brushed the hair from my forehead, kissing it. His lips came back red and I started to wonder where the Kool-Aid was before I remembered that I was bleeding heavily and that was my blood on his lips.

I knew I was dying – that there was a very small chance that I would make it out of this. I knew that right then I was wishing I really was dead, rather than going through that pain. I looked at Nate through my blurry vision and couldn't help but think that I would be happy to die right now, with the person I love. With the person who would take care of me through anything. That it was a good way to die, in the arms of someone you love. That a kiss on the forehead was a good parting gift from the world.

"Ju-just kill me," I managed to cough out between gasps, the only thing I could get out before blood once more filled my mouth and started leaking from the sides. "Please, kill m-me, ple-please!" I stuttered through the blood.

"No, Alex," Nate started saying, the tears still falling from his cheeks and onto my arm. "You have to survive. You can't just leave me here! You can't...." I didn't get to hear the rest of what he said because the small moment of clarity that I'd had was gone.

I felt his hand shake when I closed my eyes, unable to bear seeing his face. Pain was racking my body now, and every few seconds I gave out a cry. I vaguely heard Kale murmur that I should have gone unconscious by now. Ha, yeah. I wished. That would have been much better than the pain I was feeling. I opened my eyes again and Nate was still crying.

"Stop," I wanted to tell him. "Stop crying. It will only make this worse for the both of us."

I felt his body shake harder when I closed my eyes, and with blackness came the serenity.

****

I woke up to see Kale standing over me, and with a terrible pain in my shoulder. I screamed and he jumped, tugging my skin with it. Nate was still sitting next to me on the floor holding my hand, crying. Then I realize my shirt was off too but I was beyond caring. Nate moved so that my head was in his lap and I was looking directly into his deep grey eyes.

Why was I not dead? What cruel force was keeping me here, unable to deal with this great pain? Why did this have to happen to me, of all people? I would have sooner killed myself than go through that torture. At least then I'd have had a direct shot with no chance of pain unless I wanted it.

"Alex, you have to stay still so that Kale can stitch the wound," Nate said and Kale began again. I started screaming through my clenched teeth, and Nate shushed me as his tears fell faster, thicker. Every time the needle entered my skin, pain spread through my entire body.

"Can't you get her more morphine?" Nate asked and Kale shook his head.

"I only had that one vial, for emergencies. How was I supposed to know that her body would need a higher dose than a normal person?"

"What can I do?" Nate shouted over my screaming.

"I dunno, knock her out! Punch her!"

Nate looked affronted. "Did you really just say that?" he asked breathlessly.

Kale shook his head, "Just move!" he yelled. Nate put my head down gently and Kale replaced him. "I'm really sorry," Kale said to me and he punched me square in the eye. I blacked out immediately.

CHAPTER 25

I woke up in the hotel in a fluffy bed with a hot comforter thrown over my body. I pushed it off, and immediately regretted it. Pain tore at my shoulder and I groaned. I lay there panting in the fluffy bed until I saw Nate walk in with a tray of food. He saw that I was awake and rushed to my side. He was full of words that emitted from his mouth so fast that I could barely understand them:

"How are you? Are you okay? Is something wrong? Are you hungry? I brought soup. Do you need to pee? How are you?"

I responded to his rapid-fire questions with yet another question: "How long have I been out?" My voice was raspy and creaky.

Nate cringed. "Almost a week," he answered. "You got really sick after you got shot." Now it was my turn to wince. "You had a high fever and you hadn't talked at all. I could barely get you up long enough to eat anything. You must be starving."

I shook my head, vaguely remembering waking up a few times, but nothing more than a blur of pain, blood, and vomit. "I'm not hungry, but I do feel a bit woozy," I said.

Nate sighed and set the food tray next to the bed. He crawled into the bed beside me.

"Why are you embarrassed?" I asked him when I saw his ears and face redden.

They turned the color of a tomato and he stuttered to respond. "Well, ah…you kind of threw up all over yourself, and um, I was the only one willing to give you a sponge bath, so…"

I started laughing. I laughed so hard that it hurt my stomach and when I moved my hands to my stomach, my shoulder started hurting. I winced and the laughter cut off immediately. "You are embarrassed because you saw me naked while taking care of me when I was a vegetable?" I laughed.

His face reddened further. "I, uh, yeah. Well, you never gave me permission to look at your body, so uh, it was kinda awkward. Especially because you were so limp. I felt like I was bathing a dead person." He says the last line with no trace of embarrassment in his eyes. "A couple of times, I would walk in and I thought you were dead. Your breathing was shallow, but slow, and I have never been good at finding pulses." He shuddered. I reclined back onto the pillows.

"And you couldn't be dead. I wouldn't allow that," he said, taking my hand. I remembered him saying something like that when I was dying in the basement of Mr. Simmions' establishment.

I squeezed his hands and looked into his eyes. They showed deep pain, pain that came from me being hurt. From me telling

Mr. Simmions that I didn't care if I died, and that I was ready. The pain was clear in his face.

"Why would you tell him that, Alex?" he asked me, his voice nearly a whisper. "Is that really what you think?" I couldn't look at him. I looked down, but Nate gripped my chin and pulled my head up forcefully, so that I had to look at him. "Why, Alex?" he asked again, searching my eyes.

Shame burned my face red. He let go of my face and quickly rose from the bed when I didn't answer. He was about to leave when I called out, "Wait!" in my raspy voice. He turned around and closed the door. "I said it because it was true," I said, and he looked down. "But it stopped being true when we were together." He looked back up at me. "I heard what you said after I had gotten shot," I said and he looked confused. I blushed.

"Which part?" he asked, moving towards the bed once more. I shook my head. I rarely said anything of the sort to my own grandmother, whom I loved more than anyone in the world. It was hard to say when you couldn't trust yourself, when you had up a wall that kept everyone out.

But for right then, just for one moment, I took that wall down. "I love you," I said, and Nate looked startled, like he never expected to hear those three words escape from my lips. He moved to the side of the bed and sat on the edge, on the opposite side of where I was lying. Gently, he put his hands on either side of my face, and touched his forehead to mine.

"Do you mean it?" he asked, his sweet-smelling breath lingering in the small space between us. I nodded slightly, and he sighed. "I love you too," he said, and he pressed his lips to mine. This kiss was not like the many others. This kiss was powerful but not in a sexual, lust-filled way. It was tender, and passionate. It was sunshine on your deprived skin, and cold water on a burn. It was dancing in the rain on a hot summer day and feeling free no matter what happened. It was bliss.

Nate pulled back when he heard a knock on my door. I slid down underneath the covers and he opened the door. Seeing Lynne leaning against the doorframe, I frowned. She seemed to be supporting herself with the wall. She and her brother appeared to be in a silent argument. Nate raised his voice a little and I captured some of what he said: "...she can't be upset right now Lynne, it's part of the healing process and it might get to her. Her immune system is down. You shouldn't be on your foot anyway, or else it won't go away."

That was when I really started to worry. "She can come in," I called out in my scratchy voice. Nate sighed and opened the door wider so that Lynne could walk in.

Or, more like, limp in. She had a crutch underneath her left arm, and was barely walking on her left leg. I looked down at her foot to see a large, bloody bandage wrapped around it. I cringed as she struggled around the bed. Eventually, she got over to my side and sat down on the bed, leaning the crutch on the bed stand. She held her arms out and gave me a big hug. I returned it tearfully.

"How are you feeling?" she asked and I shrugged, which earned a nice wince that turned into a shudder. She laughed. "I see," she said.

I looked down at her foot again. "What happened?"

She smiled at me sadly when she said, "We were looking for food and medical supplies for you. The people who kidnapped me kinda ruined my tennis shoes. I was wearing the flip-flops."

I knew where this was going. She'd stepped on a nail, or a broken piece of glass.

"We were running away from day-walkers, and I tripped in my flip-flops. They caught up with us – me and Ky. One of them grabbed my foot and..."

I gaped. Apparently I hadn't known where that had been going. "Wh-when did it...happen?" I asked, quivering a little in fear.

"Just two hours ago," she said. I looked at Nate, horrified. He kept his head down but I still saw the tears glistening on his cheeks. "He thinks it may go away," she whispered to me gravely. I could tell she didn't believe it one bit – just like me. "I only have a day at the most," she said.

I felt a warm, salty tear streak down my face and into an unhealed cut. I hugged her again as she patted my back. "Did you tell Kale?" I asked.

She shook her head. "I told him that I had stepped on a broken piece of glass before the day-walker got me. It was a small wound, so he believed it."

"When do you plan on telling him?"

"Not until the end. Not until we have our last moments together. I already told Nate that I want Kale to be the one to end it all."

"Why?"

"Because he is the one I started living for. You know how that feels," she said, and absent-mindedly, I nodded.

"How hard was it to tell Nate that you were bitten?" I asked.

"I didn't. He was the one who cleaned the wound and saw it for what it was. The hard part was telling him that Kale and I were together." She let out a small giggle, and I laughed.

"I understand that," I said. I glanced over to Nate, sitting in the corner on the reclining chair. With my good hand, I motioned for him to join us and he shook his head. I waved my hand impatiently and he sighed before climbing onto the bed beside me. I intertwined my fingers with his. His hands were warm and shaking badly. I leaned my head on his shoulder and his arm automatically wrapped around me.

Looking back at that moment, I realize I could have done something much different. I had a gun in the nightstand. It was loaded, and the safety was off. I could have whipped it out, shot Lynne then and there, and avoided the suffering that followed. But I didn't. And I don't think I would have done it even now. It was Lynne's choice, and it was the way she wanted things. Kale would have done anything for her. I realized that I would have done the same thing if I were her. Like I have or haven't said before, this world is cruel. People die every day from terrible causes. But we just have to suffer and move on.

CHAPTER 26

Nate and I left Lynne to be with Kale for her "last day." We promised that before sunset, we would tell Kale everything. But for right now, we just let them be together.

I learned from Nate that the people who had been torturing me were outside fighting Lynne and Kale after I had passed out the first time. Apparently, Lynne had fought bravely, and even shot one of Simmions's men through the throat while he was still in the room with Nate, Kale and I. I was happy that Lynne was getting stronger in her fighting skills, until I remembered that she would be gone in a few hours' time.

Nate was sad that he didn't get to spend more time with his sister, and I couldn't say I knew the feeling, but I did understand. It was hard to lose a loved one who you knew is going to turn. It was much better if it just happened without you knowing. He was going to interrupt Kale and Lynne's evening, but I stopped him.

I used myself as an example. "If I were infected..."

"Which you won't be," he said. "I would die before I would let you be bitten by a night or day-walker."

"Okay," I said evenly. "But in a hypothetical sense. You wouldn't want to let my 'brother' have all of the time with me, right?"

He gritted his teeth and looked away. "That isn't the same."

"It's exactly the same."

"But you don't have a brother," he said. "And you wouldn't tell me."

"What?"

"You wouldn't tell me if you were bitten. You would keep it from me until the last minute."

"How do you know so?"

He shrugged. "Because I know you. You would pretend everything was fine until the last minute, because you wouldn't want anyone to worry or freak out or anything. Because you are selfless." He turned toward me again, wrapped his arms around my waist and looked into my eyes. "Because you are brave and kind and courageous and fearless and proud and stubborn and beautiful. That's how I know."

He hugged me to his chest, being gentle with my shoulder, and we sat there for a few moments, wanting to freeze time, never wanting sunset to come.

****

At around seven p.m. it is starting to get dark. I am lying on the fluffy bed, underneath the covers and Nate is lying beside me, on top of the covers. He sighed when he saw the sun starting to descend in the sky.

I turned to him. "I don't want to hurt Kale," I said and he nodded.

He knew what I meant. "You don't have to come. You should probably stay in bed anyway."

"No," I said. "Bring him in here. I don't want you to have to do it by yourself."

"Alex..."

"No. Go get him."

Nate shook his head at me then got up and walked out of the room. I lifted the covers off of me slowly, and sat up even slower. I was only halfway sitting up when Nate and Kale walked into the room, Lynne trailing behind. Nate rushed over to help me, and I gave him a grateful nod.

Kale was fidgeting, nervous. "What's wrong?"

He kept repeating this over and over. I looked at Nate, and Lynne came over and sat beside me.

"Kale..." I started the sentence, but couldn't finish it because of a lump in my throat. I swallowed and began again. "Kale..."

Lynne finished for me. "I've been bitten."

Kale looked between me and Lynne doubtfully. "Guys, that joke isn't funny," he said.

We didn't smile, or try to correct him. We just stared at him and hoped that he realized on his own.

He saw our solemn faces, our joyless eyes, but still chose not to believe it. "That isn't funny," he repeated.

Lynne propped up her ankle onto her knee and started to unwrap the bandages. She unwound and unwound until finally we saw her foot. There was a small arch, with small lines that were from small teeth. The teeth of an undead child. Kale saw the teeth marks and went silent.

"What..." Finally seeing the wound for what it really was, he couldn't finish his sentence. "Why didn't you tell me?" His voice cracked and there were tears in his eyes.

Lynne got up and limped over to him. She hugged him, and he stood stiff, his arms just hanging by his sides. "I didn't want you to worry," she said, and there was a tremor in her voice. His arms moved and tightened around her.

Nate put his arm around my waist. There were tears in his eyes. I would have brushed them away if Lynne's body hadn't decided to drop dead at that moment.

Only, Lynne's body didn't shut down on itself. I saw the blood and heard it drip on the carpet. It wasn't until I rushed over to her that I saw the metallic glint of the bloody knife sticking out of her stomach. I pulled it out slowly as Lynne started to groan and I winced. Soon enough, she would be moaning for flesh and not out of pain.

I whipped the knife out quickly, realizing that it didn't matter anymore. She was going to die anyway. I didn't need to investigate anything. We all knew who did it. I didn't need to look for the spade on the side of the knife to know it was Kale who had done it.

Nate glared at Kale through hot tears. "What the hell?!" he yelled, pushing Kale. "Why did you just kill her? She had time, at least another few minutes or so..."

"It doesn't matter, idiot," Kale interrupted with a cold voice. "She was almost dead. I would rather see her die from my doing than that of a stupid zombie. I would rather see the red staining my hands than see red staining hers."

"That wasn't the right way to do it!" Nate exploded. I shushed him and took his hands in mine.

Kale didn't have to explain, to me at least. Nate had never lost anybody of utmost importance to the apocalypse yet. He'd never suffered that pain yet. And I never wanted him to. But this was something we all had to go through. Young or old. Yes, it was tragic. Yes, it was unfair. But did that matter anymore? Did anything? What made life fair? Who said what was fair and what wasn't? Did it matter? I mean, even before the apocalypse, people had to die. People died every day. It was something that had to happen eventually.

Nate's hands shook with either rage or grief. Maybe both. Tears streaked his face as he looked down at his dying little sister. I risked a glance back to see Kale kneeling beside her head, her face in his hands. He was stroking her cheek, her nose, her chin, her lips. Wherever his fingers went, he left behind a dark red stain.

Nate moved his arms and wrapped them around me, burying his face in my hair. I felt his tears soak my hair.

"Kale," I said. He shook his head. He didn't want me to continue. But I had to. "Kale, she is still going to come back. You just quickened the process." Nate's arms went stiff when he heard me, and I cringed.

Kale shook his head more vigorously. "No, no, no, no, no, no. No she…"

He was interrupted with a moan that came from the body on the floor and he looked down quickly. He must have seen the clouded gray eyes and known that she had turned. He had to have.

Kale whipped out his gun from his waistband.

I ran over and pried it from his hands. "No," I said. "Not here. Not now. Not you." He looked at me with a half-grateful, half-mad look before nodding and sitting on the bed next to Nate, who was now sobbing at the sight of his younger sister-turned flesh-eater.

I moved quickly, finding the small ball of twine in Kale's bag and wrapping it tightly around her hands and feet. Dumping out the extra clothes, I used my pillowcase and wrapped it around her head. Then, slowly, I picked her up and carried her to the elevator and down into the basement, my arms under her neck and knees. She was trying to move the pillowcase, and even bite me through it, but struggled with her feet and arms, making it difficult to carry her.

Putting her down on the floor next to the generator hurt my shoulder immensely. She still struggled against her bonds and I left those on but I took the pillowcase off of her head. Her small gray eyes were clouded over with the "illness." Seeing a dead security guard flesh-eater, I went over and stole his gun from its hip holster. I aimed the gun at Lynne, my hand shaking. This wasn't like killing the man from the mansion in Tennessee. This was one of my own family, someone whom I loved.

"I'm so sorry," I said. "For everything."

And I shot her between her eyes. Eyes that went dark.

CHAPTER 27

I sank down to my knees beside her head, which was pooling with the leftover blood from when her heart was still beating. When it still ran through her veins. When she needed the oxygen to fill her lungs and energy to make her move. When her brain still functioned properly.

I sat there for I don't know how long, just remembering her. I remembered the way she chopped her hair short so that she wouldn't have to deal with it. I remembered her condescending tone, her snarky attitude. Her disapproving stares aimed at her brother and me.

I remembered when she showed me how to create a daisy chain – when she picked me some of her favorite flowers. I remembered when she smiled at the worst moments, because she was thinking of something pleasant to take her mind off the gory world that existed in front of her eyes.

I remembered her girly-ness, how she was scared of spiders and snakes. How she liked to wear skirts and cute shirts more than the tight, protective clothing that was mandatory for survival. How she cringed every time somebody fired a gun because it hurt her ears. I remembered how she'd been like me before this mess of a world took over.

I remembered her protective stare at her brother. Her high, twinkling laugh that rang out at the corniest jokes. The smell of her favorite rose-scented shampoo. The way her eyes sparkled when she had a surprise, or when she came up with a purely mischievous plan.

But most of all, I remembered that she was my friend. A sister. Someone to count on. Someone to trust. Someone who trusted me. And I'd shot her between the eyes. Like a heartless monster.

I didn't feel the tears slip down my cheeks. I didn't sob, or cry. I didn't move. I didn't do anything but stare at her and remember her. Because if I didn't take the time to remember, then I would forget, and nobody would ever want to forget Lynne. Smart, loyal, proud, girly, strong Lynne. A dead fourteen-year-old in a world of young people.

I was still sitting there with a gun in my hand, staring at Lynne, when Nate found me in the morning.

CHAPTER 28

I woke up in my bed, the thick down covers shielding my body from the sunlight falling through the open windows.

Even though it was very hot underneath the covers, I shivered. I looked over to Nate's side of the bed to see it empty and already made. I knew that I should get up and shower and clean my wound. But it was easier to just lie in the soft bed and pretend that what was coming in the day ahead was easy. I pretended I was back in my bed at home, not wanting to get up on Sunday because I knew it would mean that I would have to help Grandmamma clean the house.

After about five minutes, I heard the door open and turned slightly to see Nate walk in. He had already showered, and I could still see the beads of water in his hair. I was confused when I saw that he was wearing khakis and a red polo shirt that were a bit too big. He noticed me awake and rushed over to the bed.

Nate lay down and jostled the bed, and I winced. He put his hand on my cheek, and rubbed his thumb back and forth just below my cheekbone. We just stared into each other's eyes for a few minutes in silence. Grieving with each other. I finally broke the silence.

"Why are you dressed up?" I asked. When I'd tried to get it out the first time, there had been a lump in my throat and I couldn't speak.

Nate sat up and pulled me with him. "Kale and I agreed that she deserves a…ceremony."

A funeral.

I nodded in agreement and swung my legs over the side of the bed. My feet were clammy and cold, and they stuck to the cold tile in the bathroom. I showered, washing all of Lynne's blood from my knees and hands. When the hot water hit my shoulder, it was both soothing and painful.

Stepping out of the shower, I wrapped myself in my towel and realized that I couldn't dress in the dirty, disgusting clothes that I'd killed Lynne in. I looked into the mirror and investigated the angry red splotch over my left shoulder. It made me grimace. The skin was raised and rough-looking, and you could see the torn muscle and skin underneath. I looked away from it, and re-wrapped it with the cloth and tape that was stored in the cabinet under the sink.

I looked up to the mirror to see somebody who isn't me. There are large bruises covering her torso, neck and face. They were a blotchy purple, blue and green, lighting up pale, sickly skin with a spectrum of colors. I saw a cut just below her right eye, which was swollen and puffy, hot to the touch. Looking inside of her mouth, I see not only a deep cut on her lower lip which was healing nicely, but a few missing teeth. I counted 3 missing molars, both top and bottom, and her upper left canine tooth was missing as well.

I tried to recognize the girl in the mirror as me. I tried to tell myself that those bruises cover my body as well. That I looked sickly and pale, that I was beaten badly, and that there was no going back from that. Sure, the bruises would heal after a week or two, and the cuts would heal into scars, but my teeth? There was no way of getting those back. I run my tongue over the spaces where my molars were and shudder. I feel the heat of tears behind my eyes, and turn away from the mirror, disgusted with the sight of myself.

I walked into the room and found it empty. There were clothes lying on the bed. I walked over to investigate and saw that they were dress clothes. There was a regular bra and underwear set. There was a guy's white dress shirt and a pair of black slacks. And next to them lay a green dress. It was sleeveless and seemed to come up to right above my knees. I picked up the dress and underclothes and headed into the bathroom to dress. I unzipped the zipper and slid into the silky dress. It was perfect and it let my wrapped shoulder breathe. I had to leave the zipper undone because I couldn't reach it. The dress fit perfectly and it was so light that it barely felt like I was wearing anything at all. I smiled when I wondered what Lynne was going to say when she saw me, the tomboy, in a dress. Then with a pang I realized that she wouldn't say anything. She was gone.

I felt vulnerable. The sleeveless dress left my shoulders free but it also revealed the white bandages that stuck to my body with the humidity of the bathroom. It revealed the disgusting, purple, blue and green bruises that cover my body, that hurt terribly to the touch.

I dried my hair and braided it into a simple braid down my back with one hand. There was some difficulty doing so, seeing as I could not raise my left arm very high. Every movement of my left arm brought sharp pain, but pain is necessary. It tells us that we are still here, even if our friends are not.

I walked out into the room to see Nate making what I assumed was French toast, on the skillet. Lynne's favorite. I sighed into the smell and Nate heard. He turned around and took a sharp intake of breath when he saw me. He walked over and I turned around, showing him my unzipped back. He slowly zipped up the dress, letting his fingers trail over my skin.

When the dress was zipped, I turned around to see his eyes shining. I put my hands on either side of his face and pulled him into a soft kiss that had all of our feelings packed into it. Happiness, sadness, anguish, rage, grief, and love. All into a small kiss.

He pulled away and managed a small smile. "You look beautiful," he said in a heavy voice that suggested he would start crying soon. He brushed a small flyaway from my face. "Your eyes match the dress perfectly." He left his hand on my cheek and I put my hand over his and held his other hand.

A tear streaked down the side of his face. I moved my hand and slowly wiped it away. That it when I spotted the unused stereo behind him. I remembered seeing the Compact Disc case sitting on the dresser. I moved to the dresser and checked to see if the disc was inside of its case. I put the CD in the stereo and pushed the skip button until the right song number showed on the screen. I knew how to use the player because Grandmamma had one. She refused to use the AudioHolos.

I walked over to Nate and had wrapped my arms around him when I heard the song start to play. He put his hands on my waist and I leaned into him as the singer sang the lyrics. He was singing something about belonging. About knowing where you stand. About how no matter what, you stay where you are, because you know that it is the right thing to do.

The music absorbed us into each other, each word in the lyrics hitting us like bombs, being so true. We didn't necessarily belong in this world, with the chaos and carnage, but I knew where I belonged. I belonged right there, with this boy. He made me happy. He helped me and knew that no matter what, I would do anything in my power to protect him, like I wished I'd had the chance to do with Lynne. And I knew that was what he was thinking as well.

I had never thought about the lyrics to this song before. I'd had it in my AudioHolo, under the "oldies" playlist. It was an old song from when my grandmamma was my age. She loved it, and I did too. Except now it had more meaning behind it.

The song ended, but we kept dancing to the next song. We kept dancing – or swaying, rather – until the songs ran out, and there was silence. But we kept dancing because if we stopped them we wouldn't have anything to do but cry, and that wasn't wise in the zombie apocalypse.

We were still dancing when Kale walked into the room, in black slacks and a blue dress shirt, and announced that it was time. By this time the tears had dried on our faces and made the skin underneath tight. I slipped on my combat boots with my dress. I didn't have anything else to wear.

I took Nate's hand and pulled him behind me as I followed Kale to the roof. There was a nice little garden up there. Well, it had been nice. All of the flowers were dead. It smelled like winter; dead plants with the sweet fragrance of life. I vaguely recognized a dried tulip in a flowerbed near the edge of the roof. In the midst of all the dead flowers was a small figure dressed in black.

Lynne's short, choppy hair looked like it may have evened out by itself and was swept back over her forehead. Her eyes were closed, and her lips were full, with a light lip gloss on them. She was wearing a black dress not unlike my own in shape. It was knee-length and flouncy looking. She had short sleeves that were just past her shoulders. She was wearing black ballerina flats as well.

She looked pristine. Perfect. Well, she would have, if it weren't for the small, three-centimeter hole in the middle of her forehead where a bullet had passed into her brain. A bullet that I put there.

Kale cleared his throat. "Is there anything you two want to say?" he asked in a gruff voice. I assumed that he had already said goodbye.

I nodded and stepped up beside Lynne. "Lynne was-*is*-one of the only people in this world that has made me laugh and smile. She can make anybody feel good about themselves. She can tell you everything about flowers. She loved everything. And even though I have only known her for around two months, she is my best friend. And I'm sorry. For everything." I stepped back and took my place beside Nate again.

In my mind, I imagined Lynne's funeral back before this apocalypse mess. Every type of flower known to man would have been in the room with her. I imagined the large boards of pictures of her, with her parents and Nate – maybe some friends. I suddenly remembered the mental picture we took together, after she had made me a daisy necklace. I imagined myself putting it next to her and kissing her forehead goodbye. She would have had her family surrounding her, crying over her body. Then I realized that she was surrounded by her family. Nate, Kale and I? We are her family now. And we will always be there for her, even if she is not here with us.

Nate looked like he wanted to say something but if he tried then he was going to break down and cry. He opened his mouth, then shook his head, the tears falling thick and fast. Kale just nodded. He moved over to the table and kissed Lynne's forehead, then backed out of the door to the roof and went back down to his room, using the elevator.

Nate wrapped his arms around me and I hugged him back. He cried into my hair and I just held him, unmoving. He pulled away and kissed me forcefully, saying, *I love you. I won't ever let this happen to you. You are safe with me* …without ever saying anything.

I pulled back and led him out the door by his hand, leaving a member of the family behind, in a black dress. She was smiling at us and waving to our backs as we walked away, a flower in her hand.

And when the door shut behind him, she was gone, finally resting in bliss.

EPILOGUE

I watched the girl in the corner suspiciously. I still didn't trust her. Not at all. She was an invader and someone that could kill me easily, judging from the amount of skill she showed when she tried to get away. She said that she was looking for someone and I didn't respond. It was probably the other two imposters that we were holding in two other houses.

She was surprisingly calm, though she appeared to be in great pain. The boy she was with, whose name I could not catch, explained that she had acquired a near-fatal bullet wound after she'd doubled over in pain from the guards using forceful methods on her.

Her weapons, the deadly guns and knives that I was sure she knew how to use very well, were being hidden far below, on the ground. She didn't seem to care that they were gone. Her bright, green eyes watched me curiously and carefully, and I quickly became uncomfortable. She was either oblivious to my discomfort, or simply didn't care. I supposed it was the latter.

She stretched her legs in front of her and didn't try to move from her spot in the corner. She obviously knew that she was chained to the wall, and that there was no way to escape from her bonds without the key, which I had hidden in my breast pocket. Picking at the edge of her frayed, torn and bloodied gray flannel shirt, she narrowed her eyes at me.

This girl was abnormal. I could have told you that much just by her green eyes and bright blonde hair. She might have been pretty but the colors that made up her features were too alien. So she was an outcast, either by choice or happenstance. I found myself pitying the girl.

She sneered, as if she had read my mind. Perhaps she had. I didn't know anything about her but her strange appearance was enough to make anyone uneasy.

"I don't want your pity," she spoke out to me. Her voice was high and strong, no quaver of fear in her strong tone. "I don't need it. It is useless and makes me angry."

"What makes you think I pity you?" I asked her, my voice unsure. I had been ordered not to speak to her, but I guess I couldn't help it. She was just too…mysterious.

She scowled. "Don't play coy with me. I can see it in your face. It's easier to read than a book."

This headstrong girl was frightening and I supposed she already knew that. It was in her nature, perhaps. I averted my eyes and decided whether or not I needed to continue speaking with this prisoner.

"Why have you come?" I asked her, deciding that my curiosity was to blame for me not taking orders.

"I see no reason to tell you," she retorted and struggled with her cuffs. I moved the gun so that she saw that I could easily shoot her. She sneered again. "You really think I am going to be afraid of a gun after what I have been through?" She must have been referring to her shoulder wound, though it confused me. That wouldn't make her invincible.

She sighed. "My friends and I just wanted a good place to live. We figured this park would be abandoned. We had no idea that you would have these tree house things. I have to admit, they are pretty impressive, all the way up in the trees. Away from the flesh-eaters. Smart thinking."

This saddened me. They had only come looking for a place to escape the living dead that walk far below these wooden floors. The gate to the park had closed weeks ago, though before that, it had been open to anyone. I mean, it was public property. That was before the angry residents that lived in these houses far above the ground decided to close the gate to everyone else, creating a safe haven for themselves only.

"Your friends," I inquired, "the two boys that arrived with you?"

Her eyes shot open. "Yes," she nodded. "They're my friends. Where are they? Are they okay? Please tell me you haven't saved me for last."

"What?" I asked her, confused. "Saved you last for what?"

She blinked. "My death," she replied casually, as if she were talking about a new purse that she had just gotten, or a pair of shoes.

"Why, in the name of the Good Lord, did you think that we were going to kill you?"

She lifted her hands, motioning to the cuffs. "It's good to know that my friends won't die," she said and I pitied her again.

"You must know, girl, that the outcome for your friends depends on their individual actions. They may die yet. You could, too."

She looked up to me, her face emotionless. "You obviously seem to be younger than me, by at least a year." She was right. I was only fourteen and she looked way older than me. "You can't call me 'girl' if you are only a boy," she chided, a small ghost of a smile lingering on her lips.

"What should I call you, then?" I asked her.

She straightened. "Call me Alex."

"Well, Alex. Are you ready to be thrown into the thick of a battle?"

She looks confused. "Battle? Between who?"

I give her a grin. "Us, and the drug lords who want to claim this land for themselves."

Her eyes widen and then narrow into a glare. "I'll do anything to take those bastards down."

ACKNOWLEDGEMENTS

First off, I'd like to thank the readers. I worked very hard and invested so much time in this book. To know that somebody out there is reading and enjoying what I wrote and created—that means the world to me. Thank you for taking the time to read this.

I'd like to thank my teachers—Mrs. Strini, because I got your jokes. You are an inspiration to me. Mrs. Devivo, for having so much excitement and giving me my first real nickname. You two have impressed a lot upon me, and I have to thank you for that. It has carried over into my everyday life.

Mom. Oh, Mom. There is so much that I could thank you for, but I can't express it all into words. You were the first to ask what I was typing, the first to read my book, and the first to give me the support I needed to follow through. I can't thank you enough, or make up for all of the times you had to listen to me click away on my laptop. You have been my at-home manager, and that can't be easy, if I know myself. And I can't thank my mother without thanking the rest of my family as well. Thank you.

I'd like to thank Emma Nippes and Emily Schmidt, not only for giving me wacky, new ideas but for egging me on. Your enthusiasm, laughter, and support has pushed me through those days where I just felt like throwing my laptop out the window. Thank you!

To Craig Peterson, you are an amazing artist. You have captured what I imagined in my mind so well. Thank you!

Lastly, to all of the people who have helped me along the way, whether you helped inspire me to write or just showed enthusiasm for what I do. This includes my friends at Homer-Center School District—teachers and students alike—and my friends at the Homer Center Free Public Library. Thank you all. I couldn't have done it without any of you.